For Moira's Sake:
A Selkie Tale

By Cynthia Murphy Andrews

PublishAmerica
Baltimore

© 2007 by Cynthia Murphy Andrews.
All rights reserved. No part of this book may be reproduced, stored in a retrieval system or transmitted in any form or by any means without the prior written permission of the publishers, except by a reviewer who may quote brief passages in a review to be printed in a newspaper, magazine or journal.

First printing

All characters appearing in this work are fictitious. Any resemblance to real persons, living or dead, is purely coincidental.

ISBN: 1-4241-6467-2
PUBLISHED BY PUBLISHAMERICA, LLLP
www.publishamerica.com
Baltimore

Printed in the United States of America

Dedication

For Lynne Mendenhall, whose loving support and guidance fostered the courage to take this step.

For my fellow Selkies, friends of my heart, my soul, my core.

For my sisters' unconditional loves.

For my mother, who first read to me of faeries.

And for my kids, who let me read to them of the wee folk.

Acknowledgement

I'm forever grateful to Renee Claire's invaluable ability to find meaning in an abrupt sea of ambiguity.

Preface

The audience I choose for this story is familiar with the myth of the Selkie. Or more to the point, they are people who are willing to allow Selkie mythology and life to blur. Selkies are creatures who exist in the sea as seals, but when they come ashore they shed their skin and appear human. What most don't realize is that Selkie maids are not the only creatures of their kind drawn to the shores to observe—there are Selkie lads, too. They observe not only mankind, but womankind, too. What the Selkie lad has in his heart, in many ways, is more powerful and fierce than a lass's, if that can be believed.

You must understand that it is very confusing to a Selkie to fall in love with a human. They have a natural curiosity about people, something that comes from deep within. That overwhelming curiosity is something that they cannot fight, being so like us but at the same time so different. Then, seeing a kind of beauty new and strange to them, it stirs powerful feelings, often for the first time. Because, my friends, you need to understand that their world is very different from the human world. Don't misunderstand me, Selkies do know love. Love of family and loyalty are very deeply rooted concepts in their society. But when love for a mate combined with passion and desire hits a Selkie for the first time they are so struck, they often forget themselves, forget what they are, and pursue this

new desire, this new emotion, this new longing, to a disastrous end.
  The constant in a Selkie's life is the sea. It is always there and will always be part of them, always drawing them home. No matter what they feel, no matter what they discover, it's always calling to them to return. Always. It's a call that cannot be ignored.
  The existence of Selkie lads really explains quite a lot actually. Lost loves, broken hearts, fatherless children. Stop and consider the gaps it would fill.
  If you are willing to believe, willing to try to understand—then I invite you to discover this tale I am about to tell you.
  I would like to take you to Ireland in the late 1800s: the western wilds of Ireland, where Connemara kisses the sea.

Chapter One

Moira loves her cottage on the beach. The sound of the waves comforts her to sleep and greets her in the morning. Her father had been a fisherman; he had built their home near the sea at Moira's mother's urging. She wanted to be near her husband and she wanted the comfort of their home to not be far off when he brought his boat in after a long day. Both her father and her mother are gone now, but their memory is strong in her heart. They had the kind of love legends told of, both for each other and for their daughter. So Moira has a high ideal of how a man should love a woman. This gave men a deep and terrible fear. Most men did not even approach her, even though she was a great beauty—though not shockingly beautiful, mind you. She had a beautiful heart, which glows from her soul and amplifies her outer beauty. Much like a stained glass window is already a thing of beauty, but when the glorious sun shines through it, it is then breathtaking. Such was Moira's beauty.

She kept to herself most of the time, as she was a very solitary soul, quiet and unassuming. But her heart held a great loneliness, which reflected through her eyes; her deep brown eyes. They were the kind of eyes that looked like they could swallow you if you looked too deeply into them. She lived alone in the cottage her father built, but she did not go out in the boat and catch fish for a living, as her father had. She had a few sheep she tended, and she spun their wool by hand to sell for a fair price at market. She also had four hens and a rooster. She sold the eggs to her neighbors who could not be bothered to keep chickens.

When ends still did not meet, she made an occasional love potion for the young girls in town. Not a witch in the strictest sense of the term, she was rather an herbalist with the knowledge of which herbs are powerful for what. She used the varieties that were grown locally. And she only did it at all when things were very tight, and never promoted it. She even let the individual girls set the prices according to what each could afford. When things were not so tight, she often made these teas and baths for the girls for free. What they did not realize was that their own hormones were stronger than anything Moira could mix up, but Moira herself was well aware of it.

The story begins on a night she was gathering periwinkles by the moonlight. This is not an easy thing to do, but when gathered by moonlight and cast upon a maiden's bath they are said to make that maiden's charms irresistible even to the most resistant heart. As she came toward her home from the edge of the wood with her basket laden with the pale blue blossoms, she thought that the sea's voice had a sad tone to it—a tone that seemed to echo her own. As she approached the water she began to sing softly a lullaby in Gaelic:

"Arrane Ny Niee" (the Washing song)

Hushabye, my darling
Hands now I'll wash them
My handsome young one
Your body fair and smooth

FOR MOIRA'S SAKE

Clothes made of silk so fine
Each day puts beauty on you
My sweet darling, with curly hair
King of stars, blessings on you
My heart, my joy
Whatever does not grow by twilight grows at morn
Whatever does not grow at noon, by night time
Grows and puts on every grace
Each day puts strength upon you….

As she sang to the sea as her mother sang to her, the sea sounded more content…or was she more content? She did not notice the handsome stranger watching her from behind a rock. His dark wild hair was long, and wet tendrils clung to his body. His dark piercing eyes never left this beauty whose brown hair blew free in the salty breeze. As she turned and entered her cottage, the moonlight revealed that his face was streaked by tears.

Chapter Two

He held her with his eyes as the soft words passed from her lips. He came for just a look, but the maiden's song touched his soul. Her song made him feel naked and vulnerable inside, as she always did. He also felt release from a sorrow he did not know was his, and the need for her comfort. Would the touch of her hand be as gentle as her song, her hair as fine as her lyrics, her lips as moist and warm as the sea mist? He had to know…. But just then she turned and went into her cottage. He had seen many humans before but this one was special—she had always been special. Only she could make him feel this way. He almost rushed to her then, but he stopped himself. This need for her would not subside, so he would return—he would see her again.

When we see Moira again, a few days have passed. She is collecting eggs, speaking in a soothing tone to her hens.

"Maybe I should get some sisters for ya? How would that be; I bet he would like some new girlfriends."

"Moira, ya must help me!" Kathleen burst in, the chickens scatter.

Quite disgusted with her young friend, she says,"Go inside and put the kettle on—I will be there directly!"

Moira enters the kitchen, which she quickly surveys. The kettle is warming on the hearth, so her eyes settle on Kathleen.

FOR MOIRA'S SAKE

The girl's already rosy complexion was aggravated from excitement and exertion—she was now beet red.

"Now what is worth all this excitement, gettin yerself and me chickens all in a dither!"

"It's Jackie!" Kathleen has recovered her breath and calms down quite a bit, but it is easy to see she is still quite agitated.

Moira asks, "What about Jackie?" as she reaches for the chamomile tea.

"I did the little blue flowers just the way you said...but I think I need somethin stronger!"

"What on earth do ya mean?" Moira sits down at the table with a look of concern. Her hand covers Kathleen's in a small act of comfort. That small act is all it takes—the young girl breaks down. Moira is totally confused and concerned. Softly she urged the lass on, "What has happened, child?"

Through sobs, she says, "Jackie has taken up with another! What am I too do?!?"

Moira goes to her, encircling her with her arms. "There, there, dear."

"I know, if we can just get rid of that one, my Jackie will come to me!!"

"NO, no! that won't help at all." She is now rocking the girl slightly. She takes Kathleen's face in her hand and with her free hand dries her tears with the corner of her apron. "First off, I can't do that. I wouldn't even know where to start, and I wouldn't want to." Still holding her chin she looks straight into her eyes, "Listen closely: Ya cannot force some one against their will to luv ya." Kathleen begins to interrupt, but Moira tightens her grasp, "Eh now!" Kathleen settles again. "Imagine if ya did get rid of the other girl, imagine how great yer hurt would be when he still did not luv ya."

Completely giving herself over to the grief, she poured

herself into Moira's arms.

"Ssssh now. I too once loved a boy when I was young who didn't give a nit for me."

"No, Moira! That can't be, not you! Your spinnin' this ta comfort me."

Moira returned to her cup of tea. "I am tellin ya to comfort ya, but it truly happened. When I was a wee child, me best friend was a boy, his father and me father fished together." She giggled as she remembered, "We gave our mothers no end of grief with the mischief we found. His name was Sean and we did everything together. It broke me heart when he fell in love with another. But me Ma understood me heart without me sayin a word. God rest her soul!" She crossed herself.

"Oh, what did ya do?"

"I cried a lot. With time the pain became a distant memory." She rose to get more water for her tea. "I would be lyin' to ya if I said the pain goes away altogether. It smarted just a little when I told ya the story just now, but life goes on."

Kathleen got a look of shock on her face. "NOT SEAN MURPHY!"

Moira just nodded as she took her cup to the sink.

"But he is a farmer, not a fisherman…and he is not married!"

"The other girl got pregnant by a Kerry lad." Holding up one finger, then a second, "He did not pursue the sea. He and his mother moved inland when they lost his da." Finger three. "We are still friends, but he is so busy with his farm and his town friends."

Moira whispered, "I think the woman who runs the variety store fancies him."

"There is no secret there, to be sure!

"Darlin', I do not want ya to miss my point. Me ma and da still loved me. I was worthy of bein' loved, and it was their love that got me through it. Ya have friends and family. Someday ya will find someone who will share his heart with ya. Go home and tell yer ma, ya might be surprised—I bet she has a story not too different from mine."

Kathleen hugged her friend tightly.

"I luv ya, Kathleen!" Moira understood it was important to say it first in this case.

"Thank you, I luv ya too."

"Now run home, child; I need to get me knot head sheep from the hills."

The girl went home to her ma with a feeble smile and red eyes. But her heart was in one piece, as opposed to shattered as it was before.

Moira rounded up Gem, her dog and helpmate with the sheep. They hiked into the nearby hills beyond the wood and round up the sheep. They had found all but one, and the sun was beginning to go down. Bea was still unaccounted for—she was one of the older sheep and she had not been well lately. She had a chronic cough, which is not uncommon with older ones. But now that she couldn't be found, Moira began to worry. It wasn't long before Gem began to bark rapidly; his tone telling Moira that all was not well. The barking was not far off and Moira quickly found them. Bea was still warm, so she hadn't been dead long. It appeared she had just gone off by herself to die quietly. There is no sign of a struggle and no blood, but Bea was definitely gone.

Normally the thing to do would be to leave the carcass in the hills, but Bea had been more than a sheep—she was an old friend. She wasn't hard to pick up; she had been shorn for the summer. She didn't seem heavy as Moira carried her down the hill. Gem lived up to his name and kept the other sheep going steadily back to the cottage. Moira did not struggle, but she didn't go as quickly. She was very grateful for Gem. She stopped at the edge of the wood and put down Bea. She caught up to Gem and the other sheep and got them in the pen with no fight. She then got a shovel and headed back with Gem to bury Bea.

It was dark by the time she and Gem returned. She put the shovel away quietly.

Leaving her dog with the sheep, she went to the beach for reassurance in the steady waves. As soon as one retreated, another rushed forward. Bea wasn't a pet—she was old. She had been sick for awhile; it wasn't a surprise really. She kept repeating these things to herself. Her father had often said this was precisely why he did not want to farm. He was afraid he would become too attached to the animals, so he would stick to fishing. Her body was weary from the load she had carried and the hole she had dug. Her legs crumpled beneath her and she plunked down on the sand.

In a whisper, she said to the waves, "Bea was more than a beast—she was an old friend." Her hands went to her face and the tears escaped quietly. She felt a form come and kneel behind her. She imagined it was her father; she was suddenly surrounded by the scent her father had carried after a long day on the sea. She felt strong hands rest on her shoulders. She drank in their strength for a moment and then gave a start because she realized it couldn't be her da!

A melodious voice came in a whisper, "Please do not cry."

She swung around to see who it was. She gasped in surprise at the site of a naked man. His hair was long and wild and curly. His cheek bones were high and his lips broad and sensual. He had a small scar along his cheek bone. His eyes—she has never seen eyes so brown, they were almost black. At first the eyes were soft and filled with concern; then when he saw her reaction, he was filled with fear. He backed away from her.

"Are you alright? Have you been hurt? Where are your clothes?"

As she reached out to brush the hair from his face, he bolted. He grabbed what looks to be a leather bag or cloak (she wasn't sure which) and disappeared down the beach.

"WAIT, DON'T GO! ARE YOU ALRIGHT?!" then quieter to herself mostly, "I'm so sorry; I didn't mean to frighten him." Louder again, "COME BACK!"

But he was gone into the night.

Chapter Three

Moira closed the door of the post office behind her quietly and softly. She felt defeated and confused. She sat down on the stoop like she was being deflated, and the stoop was where she happens to come to rest. The post office was the hub for all the information in town, both news of the world and local gossip. The post office had a telegraph and the post mistress knew exactly whose husband was steppin' out with whom. No ships crashed on the rocks last night. When pressed why she would ask such a thing, she simply said, "No reason, really." She even listened to the entire load of current gossip so she wouldn't give rise to suspicion by having requested specific information. In the entire local muddle, there was not a shred of anything that could explain the man on the beach. So the stoop was a regrouping point for her, to try to reorganize her thoughts and decide where to go next.

Her fingers ran through her own hair. "It is just impossible. He must have come from somewhere," she muttered to herself. Suddenly she heard a wagon coming and got up, brushing off the back of her skirts. While twisted in this act, a warm familiar voice cried out, "Moira, darlin'!!"

She looked up to see a warm familiar face. "Oh, Daisy!!" Daisy was a round and hearty traveler woman. She was an old family friend—her whole family's, really. Moira's father would invite them to make camp on his beach for a few days when they were passing through.

They never outstayed their welcome. Daisy's husband would help with odd jobs, Daisy always had the most delightful stories to tell Moira, and every year the number of children they had with them was different! Some years three, then five, then two—not always increasing and not always the number of babies increased. Some years there were more older kids than the year prior. This fact always seemed to bother Moira's mother. The only fight she ever heard her ma and da ever have was about this very thing. Moira was a wee thing, and she should have been asleep; her parents were trying to keep their voices down so as not to wake her.

"I don't like that gypsy woman fillin' our Moira full of nonsense." Moira's ma had a note of concern in her voice.

"Ann, it don't hurt the girl none and she loves the old tales." Da just poked the turf fire.

She now crossed her arms and stood with her feet apart, firmly planted to help her stand her ground. "I'm tellin' ya, David, that woman has taken a fancy to Moira, and I don't like it." She emphasizes the last bit to show she was serious. "What is to prevent her from just whiskin' Moira off and takin' her on the road? Lord only knows how many of those other younguns she got that way." Here came what she had been bracin herself against.

"I WILL NOT TOLERATE TALK LIKE THAT IN MY HOME"

"Ssssshh, ya will wake Moira!"

"Which is why YOU will stop that talk right now. I will not have her hear such talk in her own home."

"I'm just scared—I can't lose her."

He gently took his wife in his arms, rocking her back and

forth and soothing her. "This is why that will never happen. Anyone would rather face a banshee than deprive ya of yer daughter." Moira crept back in bed, sleeping fitfully the rest of the night.

The next day, as soon as she was done with her chores, she snuck off to Daisy's caravan.

"Aren't you tired of me stories yet, lass?"

She was stirring a large pot over her fire, "Daisy, where did all your children come from?" Moira's angelic voice was pure innocence. It caught Daisy off guard and she snorted her tea through her nose.

"I'm not sure what ya mean, child," she said, wiping the tea from her chin. "Do ya not know where babies come from?"

"Oh yeah, sure! Mrs O'Malley got really fat last year and Ma said she was fat cause her baby was in there. Then the baby came out and I think it wanted to go back cause it cried all the time."

"I guess that is pretty much it, sweetie." She sat down on a stump to enjoy her tea, and patted her leg, signaling for Moira to sit down.

Once seated, Moira looked up into her kind face, with all earnestness she kept at it, "No, that isn't what I mean… Like Eric! He is all big, but he wasn't with ya the year before. Ma says you probably whisked him away or something. What does 'whisk' mean?"

Dais's eyes got huge with horror and then ripe with indignation, then misty with pain. "So that's what she thinks, is it now?!" Moira continued to look up at her with a question in her eyes.

"Eric is me sister's son—he wanted to see the sea. I love Eric like me own; I couldn't say no when he asked. Some summers my older girl goes with me ma and da. Each year is new and different, like petals on a flower. Now be off with ya child—I have work to do."

Moira kissed her and hugged her round the neck. Daisy could explain things so Moira understood.

The flower thing she got—she could understand that—but she still didn't know what "whisk" was or what it had to do with having babies. The next day, Daisy and her husband moved on, along with the herd of kids; between the loss of Daisy's stories and the loss of the new playmates, Moira was sad to see them go. They didn't come back the next summer, but they came the summer after that. They didn't come every summer anymore; when they did come, they only had their own kids with them. Daisy would always make a real point of introducing all the small ones to Moira's ma.

Nothing had changed. Daisy overflowed with love when Moira squeezed her. Moira needed Dais now; she couldn't quite put her finger on why, but she missed her old friend just the same. "You can stay for a few days, can't you? Please say you will!"

"A few days of the fresh sea air will do us good, that is if you will have us?"

Moira rolled her eyes. "Yer as welcome as the sea to the beach."

"Aye, ya sound like yer da, God rest his soul."

"Ya must do me a favor now. I still have a few errands to run, could ya ever stop at Mullins' Merc on the way out of town?" Getting her money out of her pocket and her list, Moira continued, "And pick up a few things for me, and get the ingredients to make that wonderful stew of yers." She got a couple extra coins out for the stew. "I will be along to help ya soon." Daisy gave her a look as Moira folded the extra coins in her friend's hand. "Now! Don't even bother."

She pecked Daisy's cheek and was off back into town. She went straight to the pub to see if any one had a lamb they would sell to replace Bea. She put the word out and did not linger—she had guests after all. Even with the excitement of seeing Daisy again, she couldn't shake the pain in the eyes of the man from the beach; her steps quickened when she realized, "Daisy will know what to do…"

Chapter Four

Moira had hurried home to help Daisy. Once she rounded the bend she saw that everything was well in hand. Daisy and her husband set up their caravan behind the cottage, offset sightly so they still had a brilliant view of the sea. She could smell the stew well before she saw where Daisy set up the pot.

Moira strolled up to the beautiful smell of the drift wood fire and the hearty stew. Daisy was humming an old familiar melody. Home felt more like home today.

"There ya are!" Daisy broke her tune to greet her friend. "Jeb took the boat out to try his luck with the fish, ya don't mind do ya?" She was referring to Moira's da's old rowboat that had been propped against the shed.

"I only hope he checked it for leaks before he took it out, I couldn't tell ya how long it has just sat there."

"Sure he checked it. Wouldn't he be more afraid of him drowning than you are!"

Daisy let out a wicked cackle. Those two were expert at teasing each other, but their love was fierce and strong. Yes, none knew Jeb's tender spots to get in a good dig like Daisy. Likewise, none knew his soft spots and just how to stroke them, as well as Daisy. The same was true of Jeb knowing Daisy.

"Now come have a cup of tea so ya can tell me of yer troubles, to be sure its hangin' in the air here, and its showin in yer face. Yer hands. Yer shoulders." Then Daisy made eye contact to punctuate this one, "Yer heart." Moira sat, and her hands were instantly filled with a warm mug of aromatic dark tea.

"I don't know if it's anything to tell, really." Suddenly she felt quite foolish, and began to blush.

"Out with it child, yer killin me with the waitin!"

Moira told her of Bea and how that brought her to the beach that evening. How she finally let go of her tears and the comfort she got from the sea. Then she told her friend of the man she saw on the beach, and how he left.

Daisy had a look of concern on her face. "Ya must tell me now what his appearance was like."

"His hair was dark and wild, and thick like the mane of a horse. His eyes a deep brown. Almost black. Yes, sharp! That's the word! And as naked as the day he was born." She half expected Daisy to be shocked by this, but it was almost as if she expected it.

"Perhaps he carried some thing?"

"Ah yes, I remember he picked up something as he ran away. I could not see exactly, but I thought it was a bag or a cloak."

"Ah yes." Daisy got up to stir the stew in the big pot, "Did yer father not tell ya of the Selkies?"

A puzzled look came over Moira's face. "What on earth is a Selkie?"

Chapter Five

Daisy turned from the stew pot with a look of equal puzzlement. Her calico skirts were blowing in the breeze, her bare feet planted firmly at shoulder width apart, her right hand on her hip, her left holding the giant spoon she used to turn the stew. A few strands of her hair had worked themselves free from her loose bun, and those few black and silver locks danced across her face. "I know yer ma, God rest her soul, frowned on yer da tellin ya the old tales, but I would have thought he would have told ya *some*."

Jeb came up with two small fish in a pail. Daisy pecked him on the cheek then inspected the contents of the pail.

"They're hardly worth the work it will take to cook em up, now aren't they?" Daisy had no pity in her heart for him today, but Moira's heart went out to him.

"I think they will make a fine compliment to the stew." Moira took the pail from Jeb. "I will just clean these up."

"Sure, if yer willing to go to the trouble, dear," said Daisy, giving Jeb a condescending pat on the cheek.

Jeb piped up with, "Moira child, let me take Gem and round up the sheep for ya, then ya can stay and talk to this one." He skimmed under Moira's jaw with his crooked finger, "Only if that pleases ya, dear." He looked over his shoulder to see if it had the desired effect on Daisy.

She loudly humphed and went back to turning the stew.

"Yer a blessing, Jeb!" Moira knew just what he was about, and her heart went out to him again.

"Right then, come on Gem, come on boy!" Jeb squatted, shaking the dog's head, flopping his ears back and forth, "Lets go get those woollies, eh?" Gem excitedly follows Jeb as he strutted out of sight, very pleased with himself.

Moira returned with the cleaned fish on long thin sticks prepared to roast. "Scoop me out some of those hot embers so I can roast these up." Daisy obliged with a large stick, and as Moira cooked the fish she turned to her friend. "So are ya gonna keep me in suspense forever, are ya ever gonna tell me what a Selkie is?"

Daisy tried to get some of her more unruly locks pinned back in the knot at the back of her neck. "The old ones tell tales of creatures that are at home in the ocean and appear as a seal. They belong to the sea but humans intrigue them. The old ones say they appear as seals but they can shed their skin, to simply bask in the sun or to observe humans closer up. They like to look at people, often it is that natural curiosity that is what gets the better of them. Without their seal skin they appear as humans, the same as you and me. It is said that whoever can catch the hide of a Selkie has them at their command. But once a Selkie finds their skin, they are compelled to return to their true form and their home, the sea." The sky began to deepen in color with the approaching twilight.

"That is the basic story, the legend has many offshoots. It is commonly believed that Selkies have the sight, and I once knew a woman who believed Selkies to be healers. Now...wait now, I can't remember if she said it was all Selkies or if it were the gift of that one in particular. But she swore she saw the maid lay her hands on a dying fisherman and deliver him from the cold grasp of death."

"This sounds like a rich story, is there more?"

"There is always more…the old ones say that if ya capture the hide of a Selkie then cut and sew it into human clothes, the Selkie will be trapped, unable to return to its true form, its skin having been altered. But the foolish people who try this run the risk of driving the Selkie mad, so strong is their yearning to return home." Gem could be heard barking and announcing their return. "Jeb knows something of the local stories, maybe over supper he will tell us a thing or two." She placed her hand next to her mouth to shout at Jeb, "WASH UP, YA BRUT, AND GRAB SOME BOWLS AND SPOONS OUT OF THE KITCHEN!"

Jeb and Moira polished off the fish, Gem getting his own bowl of stew. All were satisfied by its hearty nature. As Daisy rose to take her empty bowl in to the kitchen her husband grabbed her by the waist and pulled her down to his lap. "That was some marvelous stew, and no matter what anyone says about ya, I think you're a grand cook." He managed to kiss her neck before she scrambled up.

"Leave off, you. Moira and I were talkin of Selkies earlier. I thought ya could add a thing or two." With that she disappeared in the cottage returning with the kettle to make tea over the fire. "Perhaps ya can tell her some of the local stories?"

Jeb turned in his toe and kicked the ground and said with an uncertain expression, stealing a glance in Daisy's direction, "I don't know more than what yer da told me."

"Please tell me what ya remember…."

"Ya know yer da said the fishin has always been fantastic here. Well he believed it had somethin to do with the seals in the area. Most fishermen have a competitive relationship with seals, because they're rascals. They steal fish and mess with nets. Yer da knew they were just tryin to get along, just like the rest of us. They understood each other, and yer da felt that was the key to the good fishin. He also believed there to be Selkies livin among the normal seals out there; ya see, not every seal is a Selkie."

Moira remembered how passionate her Da had been about the wildlife. With every word Jeb spoke, his memory became more vivid. Moira asked, "Why did he feel the seals were involved?"

"One summer, some men came to this area to hunt the local seals. Besides the horrors they inflicted on the seals, the fishing was also very bad that year. Yer da led a few other local men and they rounded up the shifty ones and gave them a good thrashin, and told them never to return or the solution would be more permanent."

Daisy gave him a cautioning look that Jeb responded to with indignity. "Well, it's the truth!" After he pulled himself together, he continued, "Anyway, after that the fishin became better than ever. It was my feelin and I think yer da's, but he never would have said it, that the Selkies and the seals were grateful— indebted almost, and the bounty bein' their way of sayin' thanks."

The night breeze had become cool and before Moira realized she needed one, Daisy had already brought her a shawl. Moira still was not making the connection and she looked at Daisy. "Yes, but what does this have to do with the man on the beach… No."

Daisy quickly explained to Jeb about the man from the beach. Nodding, he said, "Well, there ya go." He yawned. "All this yammering has got me tuckered out. Honestly, Daisy May, how do ya keep it up?"

He kisseed Moira's forehead good night, but when he tried for Daisy he got her fist in his stomach, but not nearly as hard as he let on.

"You scoundrel, don't ya Daisy May me!"

Jeb chuckled and as he climbed in the caravan, over his shoulder he said, "Don't be long, luv."

Daisy looked around and saw Moira walking out to the beach. Daisy went into her caravan but returned quickly to the fire. She brewed up some tea using what she brought out, then with mug in hand caught up to Moira, who was staring out at the waves. She rubbed her shoulder nurturingly with her free hand and said, "He won't come to ya tonight, luv, not while we're here," and handed her the mug. "Now drink this up like a good girl."

Sensing something unusual about the tea, Moira asks, "What's this?"

"It will enhance the intensity of yer dreams, but ya must go to bed right after ya drink it up."

"I don't understand, why do I need this?"

"Yer da is very much apart of ya, he will always be with ya. I can feel his love for ya even now. When ya see him tonight in yer dream, ask him about Selkies."

Looking her straight in the eye, Moira took a huge gulp. Daisy reached out to her and said, "We will be back soon. Like I said, he will not come while we are here, so we will go tomorrow, but we will be back soon…Now go straight to bed and I will help ya figure out the dream in the mornin', before we leave. I will leave ya to finish the tea. Night night, luv."

Moira took another sip while staring out to sea. The warm steam curled around her face, twining into her hair. The strong aroma of roses was almost intoxicating. She eagerly drank the last drop before she turned to go in.

Daisy had underestimated him. He was there. He was watching. He had no intention of being spotted, but he was there. He couldn't stay away….

Chapter Six

Moira entered her cottage to find her bed ready and waiting for her. She kept her father's pipe on the mantle of the fireplace. As she drifted off to sleep she was sure she could smell his pipe tobacco. In reality she passed several hours in restful sleep prior to dreaming, but from Moira's perspective it was but moments. At first she just felt the sand between her toes, then when she looked down at her feet she saw a child's feet. She realized they were her own. She looked to her cottage and saw the smoke from the peat fire rising from the chimney, but it was the scent of the tobacco that filled her nostrils and her heart. She ran to the cottage as fast as her little legs would carry her and burst through the front door to see her da quietly tugging his pipe and rocking in a chair near the fireplace.

"Hey now, my wee gossum! What's the stampede about? I am always here!"

She covered half the room before he could blink, then she was airborne, jumping into his lap. Her arms were around his neck, squeezing for all she was worth.

Holding his daughter gently and lovingly stroking her hair he said, "Don't squeeze the stuffin' out of me!"

"Sorry Da, I just luv ya!" Moira grinned, though there was a tear of happiness in her eye.

"I luv ya too, Moira dear!"

The melody of those words soothed her body and soul. She buried her face in his chest and never wanted to come out, leaving her da to introduce the matter at hand.

"Moira dear, isn't there something ya wanted to ask me?"

She raised her head and he brushed the stray hairs from her eyes. It took her a moment to remember what she needed from her da other than this. "Da, Daisy told me of the legends of the Selkie and then Jeb told me the local tales and some of yar troubles with seal hunters, but Daisy told me I should ask you. About Selkies, that is."

"I know it is probably hard to acceptm but I know they're real, gossum. I know because I've seen 'em. Well, one for sure."

She was very attentive, eager to drink in his words, eyes wide and hungry, and he could see that she wanted more than anything to hear.

"It was during that terrible time that Jeb told ya of. As far as I can see, poachers is just another word for thievin' murderers. They would take the skin off a seal's back and leave the bloody corpse on the beach to rot. It was a sight that made me sick, physically. One afternoon, when I was out by meself, I saw a young lad tangled in a net—not a fishin net, a people–catchin' net, it was far to coarse for a fishin' net. So I rowed over to the outcropping to help. He was out cold, and bleeding from his face.

"Tangled up with him was a seal skin. My first thought was he was from one of their damn boats, but the lad was hurt and unconscious, so I untangled him and the skin. I realized he couldn't be one of them, he didn't have a stitch on. So I hauled him into the boat and began to row home. You and yer ma weren't home so I took him inside, and wrapped him in some blankets. He looked twelve or thirteen. While he was out I removed a fish hook from his face. It was in there deep and it bled somethin horrible. I stitched it up with yer Ma's sewin needle and then fed him some hot tea laced with whiskey.

"Slowly he came around. The first thing he said was, a very groggy 'You saved me.'" As he finished the story he reached down and tickles her feet. Her eyes follow his hands and as her feet come into focus she realized they were no longer children's feet being tickled by her father, but adult feet standing on her kitchen floor. Suddenly Moira was no longer on her da's lap. She was an adult, watching the scene before her of the young boy and her da.

"I suppose I did," says her da, dryly. "What happened to ya?"

The boy was still a bit dazed, and spoke in a very halting manner. "Something stung me," his hand rose unconciously to where the stitches were now.

"It was a fish hook, I removed it."

"I surfaced because my sight was clouded by the blood and I was…was…"

"I would be scared, tis alright to be scared."

"That's when the bad ones spotted me. They chased me down and threw that net at me, it seemed to fly." He took some more tea and continued, "But I dove under and managed to lose them. It started to become so heavy and it made it hard to swim. So I found that crag which I climbed out of the water on, but it was so hard. I kept climbing and pulling, I was so tired but I kept pulling. Then I blacked out." He began searching with desperation for something, but whether it was because of Moria's ears or his distress, she could not understand what it was. "Where is it!" the boy insisted, becoming visibly agitated.

"I'm sorry son, I don't understand. I don't understand old Irish. Please don't upset yerself."

The boy began to panic, wildly looking around. He spotted

the leather hide. He jumped up, grabbed the hide and ran for the door. He stopped before he ran out, only turning halfway to say, "Thank you."

Suddenly she was on the beach, and it was a moonlit night, the night she first saw the man—the Selkie. He was right before her. She reached out to touch him and this time he let her brush away the hair from his face.

She saw the scar along his cheekbone and as she touched it with her fingertips, a blinding light came from the scar. Moira woke with a start, clammy and covered in a cold sweat. She lay on her bed for a while but was interrupted when Daisy bounded in, ready for the day to begin, eager for the road.

"I filled yer jar with rain water. You can wash up, then we'll have tea and toast and ya can tell me of yer dream. It looks like it was a good one at that." She slapped Moira's knee and went to put the kettle on and start the toast. Moira and Daisy sit down. Moira, though washed up, was still visibly spooked, but Daisy had everything in place and she was obviously chomping at the bit to hear her dream.

"Well dear?"

"I'm sorry, I don't think I can tell ya yet."

To say that Daisy looked disappointed was only half telling it.

Moira clutched her friend's hand. "It is such a personal dream. I'm afraid to share it just yet. Let me sort it out for meself, then I can tell ya ." Moira got up and crossed to the front door to look out at the sea. "Have ya ever had a dream so real, yet unreal, it scares ya?"

Daisy placed her hands on Moira's shoulders. "I know exactly what ya mean, luv. We'll not be far when yer ready."

Moira turned to hold her friend. She needed Dais's brand of nurturing support.

"Tell me this luv, do ya at least know who he is now?"
"Yes, I do" She pulled back to look at Daisy. "I know who he is, Daisy."

Chapter Seven

Moira went about her day after Daisy and Jeb left. Her mind and her heart weren't in her chores, but she did them without thought. Her mind was busy, desperately going over and over the dream and looking for a link to a metaphor that could explain this Selkie business. When she and Gem went up after the sheep, she just sat in the grass, muttering to herself.

"Da wouldn't lie to me… He wouldn't knowingly deceive me…. The story could have represented something else. *But what*? I remember once Da removed a hook from Sean's hand… could it be that story got all tussled up with what Jeb was tellin me? That tea probably just jumbled up all those images in me mind. But then who was the man on the beach?"

When looking up, she saw that Gem stood a few feet in front of her with his head cocked. He made a slight whining sound and Moira would have sworn that he was worried about her.

"Oh, Gem dear!" She rolled his head in her hands and hugged him. "If a person saw me they would think my pot was cracked for sure," she continued scratching his ears, "but not my champion, eh!" She nodded her head to the side, and Gem knew what to do. He took off after the sheep. Moira looked up at the sky through the treetops as it turned from amber to a rosy glow, telling her that twilight was not far behind. The blue edge of the night started to creep up from the horizon.

After she got the sheep in she had a light supper, then went to sit out on the beach. The sea seemed calm tonight, making the steady sounds of contentment. She became lost in her thoughts again, weighing her dream against the cold hard world that said this Selkie stuff had to be a silly notion. Abruptly realizing that she had a chill, she ran in for her shawl and a cup of tea. Quicker than scat she returned with her steaming cup and settled back in. Taking small sips, it seemed like hours had passed. The stars were now twinkling bright. Her tea done, Moira decided to lay back on the sand and stargaze.

"Well," she told herself, "it looks like there is no Selkie. But now we are back to that man being lost or hurt." After some consideration she said, "Maybe I will pay the priest a visit tomorrow, he might have an idea who this man is."

Her mind at ease, she drifted off to sleep counting the stars. She began to make small rhythmic snoring sounds. Then, not before, just then, there was some small movement near some rocks that jutted out of the sand.

Tonight he was clothed. He'd been watching people all his life, so he "borrowed" some clothes from a clothesline. He wanted to be prepared. The last time he showed himself had been on impulse, her tears drawing him out before he was ready to be seen. He wanted to be seen this time. When he was searching the various clotheslines along the beach, he knew what he was looking for.

On the bigger ships the most impressive men, the men that everyone listened to and took orders from, had clothes with shiny buttons, and hats with shiny brims. He found no shiny buttons and absolutely no hats. He decided on a poet-style shirt that was very loose fitting. Damn, no buttons at all! Just these little tie thingies that he could not manage. Then he found some pants that only came to just below the knees, but at least they were dark blue like the important men on the ships. Now he thought he was ready. When she was still he crept out closer to her. A few feet away he stopped and observed. Her eyes were closed and her chest rose and fell as she slept. He drew closer, examining, but not touching. She shifted and released a small sigh in her sleep; it startled him but he stood his ground, or more accurately, squatted his ground.

A marvelous grin exploded across his face in an instant, as a wave upon the shore. As he sat next to her, he thought out loud in low whisper, "She is so beautiful, she must be a dream… Do I dare touch her, or will she disappear, as a dream would, if I touch her? Or, is she dreaming me—will I fade away if I touch her?" The yearning welled up inside him, and finally he could no longer resist. He lightly brushed the backs of his fingers through her hair, gasping at the sensation. His hand ran the length of her hair and cupped a curl at the end of it. It was soft as the ocean breeze, and as sweet. He grew bolder and, leaning on his elbow, he lightly rested his palm on her face. He was now completely lost to his heart. He had to taste her lips, even though a kiss would surely wake her.

He had to.

He would.

Leaning forward to gently caress her lips with his own, he found her lips as soft and firm as he imagined. He felt her take in a deep breath as she woke, but she did not pull away. In fact, he felt her return the kiss and deepen it, her hand raising to caress his face as they kissed. Breaking it, she skimmed his cheekbone, barely touching his skin with her fingertips, and found the scar.

"So you are real, not just a dream," Moira whispered breathlessly.

He spoke. "Indeed I am real, Moira, and I'm right here."

"But…but…how is it that I can understand you? How…how do you know my name? My God, your eyes—I've never seen anything like them."

His head still resting on his elbow, he stroked her hair as he answered her questions. "I have been watchin' people all me life, I understand yer language almost as well as I understand me own. I know more than yar name, Moira," Speaking her name, he seemed to be showing off. "I know everything there is to know about ya. I have been watchin' ya since ya were a wee girl." He seemed quite confident that he held all the cards.

"Ever since me da got that fish hook out of yar face, ya mean," said Moira, smirking. He didn't know everything there was to know, then.

He doesn't look quite so smug without the advantage. Her curiosity also in her fingertips, she traced his cheekbone and then his lips with her fingers. Keeping her eyes open, she surveyed the texture of his lips with her own. She ran her fingers through his long hair. It looked coarser than her own, but contrary to her expectations, it was softer.

He placed kisses all over her face as if he were trying to find every rise and fall of her skin. She gently pushed his shoulders back so she could look him in the face. "Do ya have a name?"

"Call me Bren."

"Ya' mean like Brendon?" She then let out a gasp. His hand had left her hair and both hands had found her waist. As he hovered over her, his hands left her waist and glided up her back just under her shoulders, and his arms began to encircle her, drawing her near. Her breath began halting and he completely enfolded her till she was tight against his chest. She caught her breath as his mouth explored her shoulder, the bow of her neck, and then the region behind her ear.

His voice became deeper still, and his breath was hot on her neck. "Just Bren. It's the closest your language comes to what I am called." He resumed devouring her neck, only distracted for a moment.

She felt as though the waves crashing on the shore were crashing in her head. It was all so intense, too intense, and she began to panic as he tugged and freed her blouse from her skirt, "Bren, please, slow down, please!"

"But, Moira, I need ya, I need to be with you!"

"But *we* need to take this slower." She wiggled out of his arms. "People don't just do this like this—honestly, some people do, but I am not one of those people." He saw the fear in her eyes and it made him pause. "Ya have had all this time," it started to hit him, "but I just found out about ya! I don't know if I even accept that Selkies are real and BAM!, yer no longer a phantom. Yer real and yer kissin me! What do ya want? Why are ya here?" The fear, though still in her eyes, began to fade into confusion, turning them glassy. The full depth of what he almost did then came back on him.

"I'm so sorry," he stroked her face. "I would never hurt ya. I came here for ya, I came because ya need me." Her eyes clear, the storm cloud passed. "Ya need me, Moira. As much as I need you. I can feel it," he placed his hand over his heart, then took her hand and placed it on his chest. "Can't ya feel it too?"

She rose, taking his hand. "Lets go inside. We can talk, and I can make us some tea."

She was startled when he offered resistance, "Moira," he said, uncertainty in his voice, "I am… uncomfortable… in houses."

"Trust me, Bren."

He rose to his feet. "I do trust ya," he said confidently.

Inside she made a small fire, just big enough to heat some water for tea and provide a slight glow to the room, and they talked for what seemed like hours. Moira spoke of how she missed her father. She poured her soul out for Bren, and he cherished every drop. Much he knew already, but he never let on when he already knew the details. He loved to hear the sound of her voice, explaining again. He, on the other hand, did not speak so freely of his life. Perhaps it was because he did not have the words to accurately describe it, but more likely because life in the wild is very harsh. The details of survival do not make pleasant conversation, and are not fondly dwelt upon. So mostly he listened, though he did describe different ships he had seen. Moira fell asleep during his recollection of the last night's sunset.

Bren carried her to her bed. She was so enchanting, he leaned down and kissed her forehead, and then he disappeared into the night—into the sea.

Chapter Eight

When Moira woke she was unsure if the night before had been real. Then she saw their mugs from tea near the fireplace; both had been used, both had tea leaves in the bottom. She felt reassured of her sanity and gathered the cups to wash. She stopped, and said out loud, "His name is Bren."

Her day began slower than usual; she started her chores but paused every now and then, consumed by a particular memory from the night before. It had been so odd, the whole thing. When he spoke he seemed to struggle at times, searching for the right word, but once he had found the best one to describe, the spoken word sounded in perfect harmony with the story and the storyteller. When Bren was telling her of a sunset he saw, it was as if she saw it herself.

"The sun was swollen and rich with colour. I imagined the sun was full of radiant colour, that being why it looked like it would burst. And the closer it came to the horizon the more colour escaped. When the sun touched the water it seemed to…." Bren searched for just the right word, as he held Moira in his arms, and found it. "…Melt into the water. No not just melt…" She tilted her head back and looked up into his eyes. Finding his word deep within them, he continued, still looking into her eyes, "Dissolve, yes, dissolve into the water. The more of the big disk went down into the water, the more colours escaped and flowed into the sea. I looked around and found that noone had seen it except for me; I felt as though I had been given a great gift."

Moira nodded in affirmation, snuggling in closer, feeling closer to him. "Thank ya for sharing it with me, now I feel as though I was there too."

"Ya were there, luv. Even then ya were in my heart. Ya have always been in me heart."

Moira found herself shaking her head to try to shake the fog out. Upon doing so she found she was up to her elbows washing clothes.

"Good heavens," escaped with a gasp. For she could not remember getting the wash basin or the clothes or any of it. The daydream had been that powerful. "That's quite enough of that; I *will* not sleepwalk through me life."

She rung out the clothes and threw them into a basket she used to transport them to the line, where the warm sun and the salty air would dry them- or as dry as they would ever get. As she was hoisting the linen over the line and fastening it she began to coo, then to hum the lullaby about bathing a baby, the one she sang to the sea what seemed an eternity ago. As she was humming, the words began to emerge low and quiet, in almost a whisper really.

"My heart, my joy

"Whatever does not grow by twilight grows at morn

"Whatever does not grow at noon, by night time."

She bent down to get another item to hang and as she stretched to secure it, she felt his warmth behind her as his body molded to hers and his hand covered hers to assist with the fastener. He whispered the final line in her ear, "Each day puts strength upon ya."

"Oh, Bren! " She swung around and his lips found hers; they

kissed tenderly and patiently as lovers acquainted for years. "I half believed I had dreamt last night!"

"Let me help ya finish." He was somewhat familiar with clotheslines, having raided quite a few as of late.

"Help me gather the eggs, and then we'll have our tea."

Moira was surprised at how calm the chickens were, despite the presence of a stranger. "They usually don't like strangers, they get all skittish and jittery." She has a puzzled look on her face as he proceeded to retrieve an egg from the orneriest one of the lot. He gently slid his hand between her and her nest and as quick as scat was out again. The maneuver would have been smooth, except that at the last moment his hair fell in his eyes, the hen excited by the curly strands, lunged for what she must have taken for a worm, pecking his nose. He let out a loud howl that sent the chickens into a flutter and Moira doubled over with laughter.

Bren emerged from the coop clutching his nose with an indignant look on his face. "I could have really been hurt, Moira!"

"But ya weren't right?" She tried her best to look serious but she was giggling.

She tenderly examined his palm for blood from his nose. "No, I moved too quickly, did not even draw blood. But it still hurt!" Almost pouting, he sat down on a stump and rubbed his nose.

Moira went to him and brushed the hair from his face, then bending down she kissed his nose, noticing a small dent in his skin where the offending hen pecked him. "After tea we will have to see about that hair, won't we?"

She headed to the cottage and Bren quickly followed, asking, "What do ya mean by that now?" but she'd disappeared inside. "Moira?"

Once in the kitchen she began to wash the eggs. "Yer hair keeps gettin in yer way, does it not?"

"Well yes, but I can make do."

"I can cut it for ya, if ya like?" Moira spoke with confidence as if the deal were already done, which seemed to make Bren all the more nervous. "Me ma used to cut me da's, and she taught me all she knew. I should have little trouble with yars. We can do it once we are finished with our tea. Would ya like an egg sandwich with yer tea?"

"The sandwich sounds fine…but what about me hair? I just don't know, I have never cut me hair before."

She looked at him as if for the first time. "Well, I don't imagine ya have. We'll soon fix that."

"Does it hurt, Moira?"

Hearing actual concern in his voice, she left the frying eggs for a moment to comfort him. "Of course not! I will never hurt ya!"

Now you see, this was not really a lie, for she never intended it to be painful, but the poor girl did not understand what she was getting herself into. Bren nervously ate his sandwich and drank two or three cups of tea, then they cleaned up the dishes. She dragged a chair to the middle of the room and motioned for him to sit down, which he nervously did.

Moira had a puzzled look on her face, "Now where to begin… First we will have ta get a comb through it."

Bren shot her an anxious look and Moira tried to reassure him. "We are just gonna brush it, to make sure all the tangles are free," she said, giving him a quick peck on the forehead. She'd spoken too soon, however, because this proved to be the part of the process that was a lot more involved than she'd bargained for. Bren had some nasty tangles that required a little effort to remove. Bren said very little during the ordeal. She was struggling with a nasty bit when he grabbed her wrist, not roughly but firmly; firmly enough to interrupt her relentless attack on the snarls.

He swung her around to his lap. "See here now luv, I thought ya said it would not hurt! I will be surprised if there is anythin left for ya to cut!"

Remorsefully she offered, "I'm so sorry. I will be more gentle! Just this last tangle and I can begin to cut."

"Alright, but I demand a kiss before ya make me bald!"

As they kissed she almost forgot what she was about—almost. More's the pity for Bren, he couldn't distract her for long. After she got the final stubborn tangle, out came the scissors. Bren braced himself, not quite knowing what to expect. He could hear the slicing noise the scissors made as they made their way through a hunk of hair, and he saw a lock of his own hair flutter to the ground he let out a mighty sigh that did not go unnoticed.

"I told ya it wouldn't hurt!"

He began to relax and the hair began to pile up. Before he knew it Moira was handing him a mirror. "What do ya' think?" She paused only slightly, then spoke again, "I left the length just above yer shoulders because I did not want it ta be a great shock for ya. When yer workin we can pull it back, like this." She held his hair in a pony tail with her hand. "Now I can clearly see yer beautiful face, and those gorgeous eyes… Why, tis a sin to hide those."

"Thank, ya darlin! I feel as though a weight has been lifted from me shoulders, a weight that I did not realize was there till I was free of it!" He jumped up, sweeping her off her feet. They giggled and nuzzled, feeling as though they were in their own world, perfectly content in it, with no reason to leave.

"I'll just sweep up yer hair…."

"I will round up Gem, then we can get the evening chores out of the way!" Grabbing her by the waist he drew her near. "Better yet, Gem and I can handle it, ya can just sit tight!"

"But I want to come!"

After a light dinner they wound up on the beach stargazing, just sitting in silence for awhile. Bren rested his head in her lap and she ran her fingers through his hair. Even though neither spoke, they shared the affection they felt for each other and the novelty of spending the better part of the day in each other's company. And that was enough.

After a while, Bren asked, "Why did yer friends in the caravan leave so quickly? Is everything all right? I know they have been friends of yer family for a long time. I remember them coming when yer da was still here."

"No, no, nothing was wrong! She just wanted us to have the time and space we needed to…find each other. " She told him of Daisy and Jeb and their kindness, how they reminded her of Da, or rather, the time they all spent together, and how she loved Daisy's stories.

Bren smiled. "I know, I loved her stories too. When she would tell ya stories, sometimes I would listen in." Moira stared at him, her eyes as big as saucers. "My favourite was the story of the fairy prince who falls in love with the human girl and steals her away to live in his fairy raft forever. Or does she go of her own free will? I can't remember."

"Ya can't remember because Daisy never told it the same way twice. That's the wonderful thing about her stories, they are growing and changin' things. Sometimes they seem ta have a life of their own." She caressed his face, then traced his mouth with her fingertip, "Me favorite was when they lived happily ever after." She gave him a light kiss, lingering for a moment. "They went just a little way north. She gave me a name of a town, where I can send word when it is alright ta return."

"Ya should send word that all is well."

"I will do that, so she won't worry about me."

"I mean that ya should tell her to return. I would like to meet this Daisy and Jeb. In a way, I know them already."

"My, ya seem so confident, I thought it would take more time for ya ta want ta meet more people, if ever."

"Just as long as Daisy doesn't want ta comb me hair, I will be alright!" he said, giving Moira a wicked smile.

"I said I was sorry!" she howled. "Please forgive me!" He jumped up and pretended to wrestle her, but she didn't put up much of a fight. Pinning her hands to the sand above her head he said with a wicked grin, "I will think about it!" Then he began to shower her with kisses.

Chapter Nine

After Bren left Moira's cottage that night, the terror of what was to come sank in. He meant what he said about meeting Daisy and Jeb, but he hadn't really stopped to consider either. Bren had a way of dealing with these situations; he shook off the anxiety and decided to deal with the problem when it happened, and not before. Till that time there was not much he could do.

When morning broke Moira was alone, but she woke with a smile on her face, secure in the memory of him. She hurried through the morning chores so she could get to the post office in order to get the letter off to Daisy. Record time today, and poor Gem did not understand the hurry, but Moira was clear enough when she told him to stay behind. She didn't want to worry about the dog today. When she finished she rushed off, clutching a letter that simply said, "Please come back *our* way!"

She stepped out of the post office with a spring in her step. The sun was so vibrant it seemed as though it was new for the occasion, brand new out of the box, special for this day. As she turned to head home she heard a songbird let out a twitter so sharp and so clear, it sounded as if the bird were two feet away. It was so close she could discern no direction; it was as if the sound came from all around. She looked everywhere, but she could not find a source for the beautiful song. Every tree was green and crowded with leaves; the bird could have been virtually anywhere. She began to whistle the bird's tune as she strode toward home, completely unaware of the friend waving, trying to get her attention, she was so caught in her own world of bliss.

Sean almost did not recognize his childhood friend. He had seen her as an adult, but today, she seemed as bright as the sun itself. She almost bounced as she stepped, as light as a fallen leaf. For a moment, he thought he heard music as she walked.

"Tis only her whistlin, ya eejit!" he chided himself. He was wavinh his arms, about to call out to her when—

"Oh yoo-ooo hoo-ooo! Sean, dear! *Sean,* I say!" It was that silly Joyce woman from the penny store, always fussing with herself and wearing too much perfume. But she had her good points too, to Sean's mind; more like she had some good curves. They made him overlook the generally unpleasing rest, including that she had pretty much staked her claim on Sean, which made him more than a little nervous.

He thought to himself, *I will just talk to her in a few minutes, now I will catch up to Moira… It's just that I haven't seen her in so long.*

He caught up to Moira as she strode down the lane with purpose, "Hey Moira, slow down, have a little pity!"

"Hey, Sean! Where have ya been keepin yerself?"

"Oh here and there…around… Which is more than ya can say! What have ya been up to these days?"

"Not much really…" As she dodged his question she felt slightly guilty; there was a time when she and Sean shared everything. But that was a long time ago. Everything was different now, so the guilt faded quickly. "How's Joyce?"

"Oh ya know, she's fine." They talked as they walked,

catching up mostly. She told him about Bea, which he already knew about, he'd heard talk that she had been lookin' for one or two lambs and mentioned that he might have a lead for her if she was still interested.

"Thanks, let me know if yer friend wants to let some go," she replied. As the road began to bend down toward the sea and her cottage, Moira began to feel anticipation at seeing Bren, and she knew she would have to shoo Sean off.

"Who are ya lookin for, I thought ya said Daisy and Jeb won't be along for a few days?" Sean was curious because she craned her neck so.

"Ya never know with Daisy May!" Her voice sounded out of the ordinary with a small strain of anxiety to it. "I would invite ya down for tea but I have some female things out on the clothesline and...and the house is not very tidy."

He began to say that would not bother him, but Moira cut him off before he could. "I just wouldn't feel right!" and she shooed him back up the lane.

Sean, starting to feel unwanted, gave in. "OK, OK! Maybe another time! Alright I'm goin'!"

Shuffling up the lane he heard her light footsteps at a running pace, retreating into her cottage. Just as he was about to round the bend, he stopped himself. He could not remember if she wanted him to ask about one or two sheep and he decided he must ask to be sure. An excuse, but he wouldn't, nay couldn't, accept a brush off.

He briskly approached the cottage door, which Moira had disappeared into, and just as he raised his hand to knock he heard her melodious giggles coming from inside. His hand froze. He was shocked at himself for the reaction, but it was as if he had no control over his actions, and he pressed his ear to the door to eavesdrop on his dear childhood friend.

"Bren stop, that tickles!"

He took a sharp step back. At first his face was covered with sheer surprise, and then realization took over his countenance. Then a concern came over him. Or was that jealousy…

Chapter Ten

Bren and Moira were playfully tickling and wrestling, then Bren realized his advantage and seized the opportunity!

"Bren stop, that tickles!" Moira shouted it out between giggles, as Bren had his way with her rib cage. When his tickle frenzy subsided the tables turned; she found his tickle spot, just above his tummy.

Suddenly he couldn't take it any longer, crying out for mercy, "OK, OK, I surrender!" They lay entwined on her bed, Moira nuzzling Bren's neck and ear, he rubbing the back of her leg. "I do prefer this."

They drifted into a nap together, Moira slipping into a dream. Her ears were filled with the sounds of the gentle sea, and the lapping of the waves was almost hypnotic. She and Bren were swimming together, but still in a close embrace, their arms and legs moving in perfect unison. He pointed to the sky, drawing her attention to the clouds. The sky had grown dark and the clouds were rolling in. She looked to his eyes for answers and found his familiar loving eyes, but surrounded by a seal's face. She was not scared and she could still feel the closeness of their bodies. As the sounds of the sea became angry, she pulled even closer to Bren.

She woke to the sounds of him knocking wood about, trying to start a fire. "I thought ya might want tea when ya woke. "

They enjoyed their tea quietly; they had discovered that they found equal enjoyment in the quiet moments as well as talking. Moira broke the silence, pleasant as it was. "I expect Daisy and Jeb will be here in a few days. Not long I suspect, she is anxious to meet ya."

Noticing that Bren looked a little off colour, she leaned in and felt his head. "Are ya feelin alright? Ya don't look so good."

"I think I just need a swim." Bren rose, leaning on the table. "I will come with you, a swim sounds nice…"

"No, no. I won't be long." Bren was out the door even before he finished.

The quick retreat slightly stunned Moira. She just stood in her kitchen, wondering what had happened. Finally she decided that Bren was quite capable, after all he said it wouldn't be long. "Surely he will be back before Gem and I go to fetch sheep," she said to herself, so she set about filling what remained of the day with small tasks. When she couldn't put it off any longer, she and Gem went up to get the sheep. It never seemed to take as long to get everyone rounded up as it seemed to take that night; the sheep seemed especially difficult and uncooperative. Really, however, they only reflected her own uneasiness.

Twilight became evening and evening melted into night, with no regard for her desire for time to stop its onward march, or for Bren to return. Her sleep was fitful and uneasy, though when she woke she could not remember any specific dream, just a general unease.

The sun seemed muffled that day. The sheep seemed in a foul mood, the chickens disagreeable too. But really she was still in a bad temper, and it colored her world.

She was taking still damp clothes off the line and replacing them with dry things, going about her daily routine, her mind filled up with other things. She was preoccupied with Bren. Clutching his shirt as she took it off the line, she stared out into the sea and softly muttered, "Where could he be? God, let him be alright." She was so intent on listening to the waves for her answer that she did not hear Sean walk up behind her.

Moira nearly jumped out of her skin when he spoke. "Have you gone and fell in love with a sailor, Moira?"

"God in Heaven, Sean, you gave me a start!"

"I'm sorry I frightened ya, but I don't think ya would have heard me if I had been singin' 'Danny Boy' at the top of me lungs."

"Eh, now—there's a thought that will curdle milk!"

Sean feigned indigence, "Hey now, I have a fine singin' voice!"

"Sure ya do!" she said with a condescending tone in her voice. "You can come in for a spot of tea," she paused, raising her eyebrows, "only if you promise not to sing! Oh, and grab that basket now would ya." Lugging the heavy laundry basket, he followed her inside.

Chapter Eleven

Like a good hostess, Moira served the tea. But still her mind was elsewhere; searching, longing, amid the waves of the sea. She was brought back to reality by the clank of a spoon landing on a plate, and caught Sean giving her a concerned look.

"So Sean, what brings ya down to the beach today?" She bubbled less brightly than she imagined, hoping to cover and change the subject.

"Can't I just visit an old friend for tea?" It was her turn to give him a queer look. "Now that ya mention it, how many sheep would it be that ya would like me to ask around about? Hmm?" He desperately tried to make this simple question seem like a weighty matter worthy of being discussed over tea. "Are we talkin about a replacement for Bea or are ya considerin' expanding?" He took a long drink of his tea, quite confident that he had drawn the issue out far enough. "I do think it's time ya thought of increasing yer live stock, ultimately to increase yer income, so ya can drop all this potion nonsense. It can't really provide that much income," he stammered, setting down his cup with a clink, "and people are beginning to talk that maybe yar, or are influenced by…a gypsy witch."

"*Sean Murphy!*" Moira didn't know if it was the words or their source that hurt her more. "You should be ashamed." She gathered herself and then carefully considered. "Ya mean to say, *Joyce* is sayin those things, and that yer feelin' the pressure!"

"Now there, Joyce is not the only one who is concerned about this!"

"Concerned! *Joyce?*" She consciously stopped herself from swearing at him. "Ya mean snoopy gossips! There was a time when ya didn't care what the likes of Joyce Shaw thought!"

This was not working out as he intended at all. He boldly tried to change the subject, wanted to talk about something that would make her happy. He already knew the answer (once again thanks to Joyce), so he thought it would be a surefire way to change the subject, "Have ya heard from Daisy and Jeb lately?" When his inquiry was met with silence and an icy glare of suspicion, he had to scramble to save the dying friendly atmosphere. "Honestly, Moira darlin, the sheep are just a small detail. I really came to visit with an old friend!"

She looked around the room, then dramatically gestured to herself, a mocking expression on her face.

"INDEED, ya ninny! Now quick, tell me how Daisy and her man are."

"Funny ya should ask, I am expecting a visit from Daisy and Jeb any time now."

The talk lightened and drifted to memories filled and coloured with Daisy and Jeb. "Do ya remember the great old story she used to tell about the Leprechaun Derby?" Sean asked, a glimmer in his eye and a smile on his face, remembering the old tale.

Moira looked puzzled for a moment, then it all flooded back. "Ya mean the one where they rode roosters!" They both laughed heartily at the memory.

"Then one tried to cheat the others…" As Sean tried to recount the story Moira helped with details he had forgotten, but then her mind began to wander.

She remembered about how Daisy said they wouldn't be far, that they would return as soon as they got word. Then she thought, *They should be here soon… I hope Bren returns before they arrive. Maybe he left because he was nervous about meeting them after all.*

Just then Sean stood up to strut around, doing his best rooster impression. As he strutted crowing she had a horrifying thought. "If the mention of Daisy and Jeb made him run, what would the sight of this one do to him?" Sean cut loose with a low warble.

She jumped up from the table and took him firmly him by the elbow. "I hate to rush ya, Sean, but, I have simply lost track of time and I have so much to do, so many chores." She shoved his hat at him, and in a second had him practically out the door. "And I must get the house ready for company. Bye, Sean dear!" and she slammed the door on his confused face.

She went about her normal routine, all the time hoping Bren would just turn up. But the sheep were in and the stars were twinkling, and still no Bren.

She stood on the shore watching the waves crash, "Me heart is breaking—can't he feel it?"

As she clutched her shawl and pulled it tighter around her, she was being watched. But this time it is not from the sea. Up at the crest of the dunes, Sean's concerned face could just barely be seen, peeking out for a look.

"She looks so troubled, pacing, waiting for someone. But who? Could it be the man I heard her with that day I saw her at the post office? I wish I had seen his face… I never did see him, did I?" Sean withdrew slowly and headed home. "I just wish I could help her."

Moira listened to the waves, but found no comfort there. Her heart was breaking anew, and having felt the dull ache in her chest all day, it had become a crushing pain. She could feel an icy cold creeping up her legs and her grip on her shawl loosened as she became consumed by the pain, and the need to recover something lost. She did not notice as the breeze stole her shawl or as it was lost to the waves. She knew that the sea held the secrets, and her feet began to feel numb but she did not care, dismissed the thought as soon as it registered. The excruciating ache in her chest drove her on to find Bren, and her heart, which he took with him. The spell of the beckoning waves was broken only by Gem. His barks had a sharp edge that warned of danger, and it was that edge that sliced through the hazy fog of pain that clouded Moira's senses. She gasped, realizing that she had waded out into the water and that it was up to her thighs. Her skirt and petticoat had floated up around her waist. They looked like the big fluffy clouds that came before a rainstorm.

    She waded back to the shore and patted Gem on the head. "Thanks for calling me back, boy." Gem whined as his mistress withdrew into the cottage, her heart heavy.

Chapter Twelve

"Yer gonna sleep the day away!" Daisy May's voice sang as she bounced on the end of the bed. "Ya best get up before I fetch a pail of cold water from the sea to dump on ya!" She tore the covers off as Moira clutched at the blanket, trying to catch the quickly disappearing corner, with no luck.

She burrowed under her pillow. "I am not amused."

"Come on now!" Daisy slapped Moira hard on the rump, moving toward the curtains and jerking them back to let in the cold light of day. "The day is goin to waste!"

"Alright, alright!" Moira somewhat reluctantly pulled herself out of bed. "Just let me wash up first," she said as she shielded her eyes from the intrusive sun, and made her way to the water barrel.

Daisy already had tea on, so now as she began to search for a loaf of bread or some such she took a step back and began to survey the small cottage. *Oh my*, she thought. It was not exactly filthy, just unkept. Daisy strode outside to find Moira and found her standing over the water barrel crying softly, tears slowly escaping down her face, but making no outward sound.

Daisy rushed forward, drawing her friend in her arms and stroking her hair, "Ssh luv, ssh." She gently led Moira into her own kitchen and sat her down, kneeling beside her. "The sorrow in yer eyes is overwhelming—share it with yer old friend Daisy May."

Holding back her tears, she tried to lose herself to the emotion. "Daisy, he is gone, and I don't know why or where or if he is alright."

"Who...who's gone, darlin?"

"Bren."

Trying to be patient, Daisy put Moira's head on her shoulder, hoping to share her burdens. "Darlin, is Bren the man from the dream? Did yer da reveal him to ya?"

"Da told me the story, or I saw part of the past in me dream, I'm not sure... then he came to me...and it felt like we had always been together...."

"Slow down, child. Why don't ya start by tellin me the dream." Daisy grabbed herself a chair and a cup of tea. Settling in, Moira recounted the dream. Daisy May sat there, wide eyed but quiet, drinking the dream in while sipping her tea. Just as Moira was wrapping up her tale Jeb popped his head in

"Tea on yet!" Jeb's bright manner instantly shrunk when he saw the serious look his favorite women were carrying.

Up like a shot Daisy was at the door "Hunt something up in the caravan, *fend for yerself*!" she bellowed, slamming the door. "Now go on, luv."

"Then he came to me, out of the night, out of the sea, he came to me. He is real, Daisy, he is real!"

"I never doubted it for a second, luv. But ya say he is gone now?" Daisy played with a stray lock of her hair nervously.

"He left two days ago, he said he would be back soon,...."
" This time the tears would not stay contained. Once again cradled in Daisy's arms, she wept, "Oh Daisy, I feel like a silly child crying over a boy, but he is real and he was here, and he made me feel..." Moira trailed off.

"What did he make ya feel, child? Ya can tell me anything!"

"He made me feel beautiful and unique and…" she paused, giving Daisy an uncertain look.

Then Daisy gave her an expectant look, her heart screaming, *Come on already!*

Moira seemed to hear, so she replied, "Not so alone!"

"Oh dear one! Ya are never alone!" Daisy felt an old familiar ache in her heart as she choked back the truth.

"It has been awhile since Ma and Da were killed, but this summer has been worse than the others, the feeling was creepin' on me like a black tide that just would not relent."

"Jeb and I will always love ya…."

"I know that, I do. I know that in my mind. He answered a need that came from my heart."

"And another thing, ya are beautiful and unique! Don't ya know that?"

"There it is again. I know these things in my mind, but my heart feels incomplete."

"And he completes it for ya."

"It's like when we were together he filled lonely spots in my soul that I didn't know I had, but now that he is gone…"

Daisy finished her thought for her. "They won't stop hurtin." The silence surrounded and affirmed the simple truth of it. Daisy continued, "Why do think he left?"

"I am not sure. He said he wanted to meet you and Jeb, but I think it overwhelmed him."

"Ya may be on to somethin there. A Selkie is a terrible shy creature. It has a child like innocence really—"

"But there is more to it than just that, Daisy. I mean to say, it is more complicated than that, he is more complicated, or his innocence is more complicated… Oh, bah! I don't even know what I am sayin any more!"

"Ya probably understand better than ya know, dear one!

Now try to explain to me again."

"Yer right about the child-like innocence, but behind that lurks emotions and needs that aren't childlike at all," Moira said, which brought a concerned shadow to Daisy's face. "I just mean he is more complex than a child, you have to wrap in survival and all the complexities of living in the wild. Just survival in general."

Daisy was still not convinced she embraced the whole truth yet, so she added, "Even I almost lost sight of it, dear, but he is not a pet. Ya need to remember that a large part of him, or how he lives, is wild animal!"

"Oh Daisy, he is not gonna eat me alive!"

"Be sure he doesn't eat yer soul or rob ya of yer very heart!" Daisy drew her near and tight to try to protect her. What Moira did not say was that she feared she had already lost her heart. These words were left unspoken, and the two held each other for a while.

Chapter Thirteen

Daisy and Moira shared the silence that only kindred spirits can share. Moira found resolve and took with her a little strength from Daisy's arms. "I must decide what to do next. I can't go on waiting, not living…"

Daisy grabbed her again in another hug, this time trying to hang on to something precious. "I will not leave ya again! I can't go, my feet won't leave yer side."

"But Daisy, I have to ask ya ta go. It's the only way he'll come back, then things can get sorted out from there."

Daisy looked on the verge of tears. "We won't go far, we'll camp at the empty field on the other side of town. Just send for us and we'll come quick as scat."

"I hate to ask ya to leave, but I fear it is the only way…." They walked to the cabin door with arms linked.

Poor Jeb stood with the horse filled with expectant worry. Daisy leaned into her friend. "Ya don't need to explain yerself to that one, I'll explain it all to him on the way across town." Daisy held her again firmly. Stroking her hair, she kissed Moira on the forehead. "We're no more than a holler away if ya need us!"

"I know, now scoot."

As soon as Daisy was by his side, Jeb was begging to know what happened. "We are going to set up on the other side of town, I will tell ya the rest when we round the bend, now turn and wave again—this time give her a smile." They waved to Moira and then rounded the bend. As soon as Moira couldn't see or hear them, Daisy let loose the flood of anger she was biting back. "Damn David, damn him and that potted plant he married, too!"

"Now luv, don't speak ill of the dead!" Jeb tried to smooth her well ruffled feathers. "Especially yer dear brother, and Moira's mother wasn't all bad."

"I warned him! I warned him! Because he never told Moira she was a traveler she's all conflicted inside! Her confusion comes from being part-traveler and part settled." She jabbed Jeb in the chest with an outstretched finger for emphasis. "But the poor child doesn't even know that much! So that Selkie is takin' advantage of her state!" Jeb started to interject, but only just got his mouth open before Daisy was off again in response to what she was sure he was about to say. "Maybe he doesn't mean to take advantage, but he is! AAHHHGGHH!" She grabbed her foot and hopped to a stump by the side of the road, clutching her foot and crying with more intensity than the rock called for.

Jeb kneeled beside her, stroking the length of her hair. His forehead rested on hers as he spoke softly in Gaelic to her, calling her his precious treasured one. Which caused her to melt into his arms. Jeb continued, "Are ya bleedin?"

"No, but the rock was sharp and it left a nice dent in me foot. It's sure to bruise up real pretty."

"Ya know if David were still here I would give him a good thrashin for makin' ya cry."

Cupping his jaw in the palm of her hand, she smiled. "I know ya would luv!"

At that perfect moment, Sean came around the corner to see

Jeb, looking like he had been drawn through a knothole, and Daisy, whose face was streaked with tears. Sean rushed forward. "Mrs. Cleary are ya alright!?!"

"Sean dear," her voice lightened, recognizing the young boy grown into a man. "I just stepped on a rock wrong, I'll be fine." She held up her foot to show that there was no blood.

Jeb rose to shake his hand. "Sean Murphy, tis grand to see ya again!" Daisy rose also, wiping her face with the back of her hand."

"I had hoped to catch ya as ya came through town. I know Moira is looking forward to yer visit, I'm a little concerned about her."

Instantly Daisy's guard went up and Jeb sensed her tension, and recognizing her body language he assumed the role of big dumb man.

Daisy was careful to keep her voice very measured. "We just came from there, and she seemed fine, darlin'." Moira had not mentioned Sean, so her instinct was to not give any thing away while getting the most information out of Sean without raising his suspicion. "Why are ya worried, darlin?"

"She has just been acting odd lately."

"Odd how, hun?"

"It's probably nothin', she just will be so happy one minute then the next time I see her she seems on the brink of tears. And she always acts the opposite of what I expect...."

Jeb let out a snort as he checked the harness on the horse. "Ya mean she is like every other woman in the world."

Sean removed his cap and scratched his head. "I see yer point."

"It was lovely to see ya again, Sean, but I would like to get the caravan settled before dark."

"Ya mean you're not going back to Moira's?" Sean pointed

back down the road the way they came.

Jeb just couldn't pass it up, with his arm extended in front of him. "The caravan would be pointed in that direction."

Daisy saw the question in Sean's face and offered a partial truth. "My hip has been bothering me, and the damp sea air only aggravates it, so we will stay on the edge of town. We will be around for a few days, I'm sure we'll see ya again."

"Not to pry, Daisy…but do you think Moira has a man?"

She paused, considering her answer. "Why no child, no one special I know of. Why do ya ask?"

Sean was unsure of himself again. "No real reason, just curious I guess. I look forward to bumping into ya again."

As Jeb and Daisy made their way up the road Daisy called back, "Bless ya, darlin!"

To the onlooker Sean must have been a sight, standing in the middle of the road, with his cap in his hands, muttering to himself. "No man?" He scratched his head again. "Daisy would know, if any one would. I never did see any one… It would explain a lot. Is it possible that Moira invented a companion in her mind?" Sean just stood there in the road, as people passed, unmoving in his concentration.

Chapter Fourteen

The sound of breaking glass pulled Sean back to reality, out of his deep concentration. He had managed unconsciously to wander to the side of the road and was leaning on a low wall. A dispute rumbling over by the source of the clatter had startled Sean. In a booming voice he could hear someone shout, "YOU CLUMSY SOD!!"

He paid little notice to the emerging conflict outside the pub. Instead he noticed that indeed the sun had sunk below the horizon. He was suddenly filled with a great dread for Moira's sake. He took off running, not really knowing what he feared or even what he thought he needed to say. He had come to the conclusion that Moira had no man, more likely he did not want to believe there was another man. But all his instincts told him something was wrong.

When he came to her cottage door, he began too knock with a heavy hand and it swung open against his arm, because it had not been latched. The cottage was empty and dark. Sean stepped in and immediately saw that the back entrance was wide open, and through it he could see Moira standing on the beach, looking out to sea. As he approached he saw that she was clutching her shawl with white knuckles. She looked like a sailor's widow, waiting for her love to return.

As he came up behind her, he touched the side of her neck

and brought his hand to rest on her shoulder. She turned quickly, and sharply. The joy in her quickly drained when she saw it was Sean, and she let out a heavy sigh.

"I am sorry, ya look as if ya expected someone else." Sean tried to hide the pain her disappointment caused.

Moira, exasperated, replied stiffly, "Oh Sean, do go away," but hearing her own voice she winced and immediately regretted her careless words.

Unable to mask the pain, it came out of Sean's mouth as anger. "Not until ya come inside with me, before ya catch yer death from this damn cold wind!"

He put his arm protectively over her shoulders and led her back to the cottage, securing the door behind them, then rushed forward to close the front door. Moira plunked down hard in a kitchen chair and slumped against a chill, a chill that seemed to come from her own heart more than the air in the room.

"I will stir the fire in the hearth to get it goin strong again." His words still conveyed bitterness and dejection. "Then I will *'go away'*."

"Sean, I am so sorry!" She rose from the chair but he already was crouched next to the fireplace. "Thank ya for calling me back, I was colder than I realized. Please, I did not mean it to come out like that."

Still half-kneeling, he turned in her direction, his voice softer, the sharpness gone—but not the sorrow, "There, this ought to warm ya up soon enough." Standing, he dusted off his hands. "I recommend ya get some hot tea in ya. I'll be goin now."

"Don't look like that, Sean!" Despite that inner voice telling her to let him go, she reluctantly pleaded, "Please stay, for a cup of tea…"

"If ya are asking me to stay for tea… I may be able to spare a few minutes."

"Make yerself useful then, put the kettle on the fire. I'll get the tea."

She busied herself looking for everything to prepare tea. "Ya know how some things tumble out of yer mouth, and yer not sure where they came from? Please forgive an old friend." She paused in her task, looking expectantly at Sean. He was turned with his back to her, placing the crane with the tea kettle over the flames.

He looked over his shoulder, his eyes a little glassy (but not to the unfamiliar eye), and said "I already have." It was at that moment that Sean's heart made a decision. Silently, what he truly said was, *"I would forgive ya anything."*

Take a step back…. No one in this story will emerge unscathed. Each individual will experience pain. I point this out because in order to understand this story, it is necessary to understand that there are no villains here. Each character has it within themselves to be a hero or a villain. From this point on, no one can escape the changes about to enfold them.

Moira sat in her Da's old chair and Sean sat on a stool near the fire, giving it a poke now and again. A silence fell in between them; not an uncomfortable or awkward silence, but that of two people who know each other very well. Occasionally the fire popped or fizzled, and then there was the constant sound of the muffled waves outside…. Sean did not even notice when Moira began to breath rhythmically in a deep restful sleep. Only when she snorted did it occur to him that his friend was dozing peacefully, and had been for a while.

Amused by her sounds of slumber, he quietly got a cover from the bed and tucked her in the chair. Leaning over the chair, he noticed that it still smelled of her Da's pipe tobacco. "I will leave her for ya to watch over, Mr. Donovan," he whispered. Quite sure that she was sound asleep, he gently kissed her forehead and, securing the door behind him, he headed for home.

But he forgot his hat; truth be told, it was on purpose.

Chapter Fifteen

It had been a long day. The kink Moira had in her neck from sleeping in the chair would not relent. She thought that certainly the walk into the hills to gather the sheep would help to work the knot out, but no such luck. Daisy had spent the better part of the day helping her friend with chores and such, but talking complete nonsense. Daisy wanted to open up the subject of Moira's identity, the nature of their true relationship, but she was unsure how to do it. So Daisy kept talking in circles all day. Moira could tell there was an underlying point to all the gibberish coming out of Daisy May's mouth, but during the walk in the hills, to round up the sheep, Daisy was unusually quiet.

Moira leaned down to Gem. "Go get those woolies. boy!" She rose with her hands supporting her back, "Let's let Gem do most off the work tonight, so you and I can have that talk you've been meaning to have all day." She raised her eyebrows.

"Oh dear, am I that obvious? I was tryin' to work up to it slowly."

In a kindhearted manner she teased her friend. "Now I know why Jeb is always sayin he is afraid ya'll talk his leg off." She giggled and Daisy stuck out her tongue. "Now I know how he feels!" She quickened her step to escape a deadly pinch.

"It is so good to hear ya laugh, I hate to end it."

"Daisy May, just tell me."

"OK, please sit down with me, I think I will need to sit down." They found a log that did the trick. "Do ya remember when your parents left this world?"

"Of course."

"What do ya remember about the funeral?"

"I don't remember what was said... but I remember everyone being so sad, Grandma never stopped cryin', it wasn't hysterical cryin' or anything, but she never stopped. In fact if ya didn't look at her face ya would never know she was cryin'. Her shoulders didn't shake, she made no audible sound, but the tears never stropped falling." Moira looked at Daisy expectantly, waiting for a contribution.

"You mean yer mother's mother? She was an odd one."

"I felt so... like I couldn't cry for my own parents..."

"I'm sorry I wasn't there for ya, luv."

"But ya were! I remember...."

"No darlin', they said they tried to find us but didn't track us down for weeks. When they did tell us David and Ann were taken from this world, ya had been with yer grandmother a few weeks. I suppose she meant well...."

"Do ya mean how she took me in for a few years after Ma and Da were gone? Yeah, to be sure, I understood why she felt I should stay with her a few years, but there just before she passed away I started to feel like a prisoner."

"Did ya know we tried to visit ya?"

"You mean at Grandma's?"

"We came as fast as we could after we heard of the funeral, but when we got here, David ...and yer ma were already planted. Yer grandmother turned us away," Daisy cried, describing her feelings of desperation. "All I wanted to do was hold ya, and try to help ya understand that scary time, but I couldn't. They wouldn't let me." Even as the tears streamed down her face, the defiance gleamed in her eyes, and a dignity shone through.

"Why," Moira said, clearing her throat, wide eyed, "why would she do that, I don't understand."

"I think we scared yer grandmother, maybe we scared yer ma a wee bit too."

Moira scoffed impatiently, "*You and Jeb*? How daft!"

"Not just Jeb and me... David's whole family scared them... yer da's family scared them."

Completely blindsided, Moira heard Daisy but still couldn't quite get her mind around the whole thing. "What are ya sayin?"

"Yer da was me brother." Daisy's words echoed into moments of silence. "Ya are Moira Donovan, a settled traveller."

Moira took it in, sitting utterly stunned, and barely breathing added the sums in head. *Click, Click, Click.*

"Please say somethin' child," pleaded Daisy, desperate, but whispering.

Moira almost startled her when she finally did speak, "It makes a lot of sense, actually. Answers a lot really."

Daisy engulfed Moira in her arms. "Oh, I was so worried! Terrified ya would be angry! I even imagined ya might hate me for telling ya who yer da really was!"

"Wait a minute," said Moira as she pushed Daisy back, "ya knew all along! Why didn't ya tell me!"

Chapter Sixteen

Sean meant to stop by for his hat earlier that day, in fact he wanted to time it about teatime. But the day had gotten away from him and by the time he got cleaned up, the sun was going down. He wanted to make out that it was an accident that he left his hat, and that he just happened to remember it...but we all know that's not the case. As he approached Moira's cottage he started to become slightly nervous. He was unsure of what to say, he so wanted it all to seem casual and innocent, but he was not very good at lying so his palms began to sweat.

"Alright, I'm here now." Sean hadn't made a habit of speaking to himself, until now; nothing much to say really. If he'd stopped to think about it he might as well have been worrying about his own mental well-being. Moira's behavior had been odd lately, to be sure. But if he examined his own behavior with the same scrutiny, he might not have been so comfortable judging her. "I will knock on the door, she will answer, and one word will just follow another," he told himself. "After all, tis just Moira."

He knocked, but his friend did not come to the door. He knocked again, still no answer, and when he went to raise the latch he noticed just how wet his hands were, and rubbed them on a pant leg. He tried again this time he was sure the door was secure. "I will just walk around the cottage and check the beach,

she is no doubt watching the sun set…"
Just as he came around to the back, he stopped dead in his tracks. He rounded the corner just in time to see Moira run into the arms of a naked man. He composed himself and stepped back behind the corner, and took a deep breath. He eased one eye very slowly around the corner. Moira and the man, he assumed to be this Bren, were now passionately kissing. He could not bear to watch. The rage of jealousy returned. He felt as though his head would explode. He eased around for another look, but this time Moira and Bren had disappeared inside. Leaning back on the cottage he lost the desire for caution and bitterly spat out in a normal tone, "Feck the hat!"

Chapter Seventeen

Bren cradled Moira in his arms as they crossed the threshold. They unmistakably expressed their hearts, using lips and tongues but no words. As they kissed their passion and need grew, as the wave that crashes on the shore begins as a small ripple. Once it reaches its destination it crashes on the beach with such might that it leaves an imprint, altering the seascape. Such was the love that grew now between the lovers, and had been building since even before they met. They became intoxicated by each other, or perhaps the intense need between them was the intoxicating agent. Whatever the catalyst, nothing existed for them outside that moment; even their immediate surroundings fell away from their perception.

This was what Bren felt when he first kissed Moira, but now she was lost to these feelings too. Unlike that first encounter, now when caution warned those thoughts were snuffed out and forgotten before the smoke cleared. She physically felt him part her legs and they instinctively entwined his waist, pulling him into her. She felt her blood racing through her veins, her skin glowing from the warmth. She could not decide if her blood was actually warmer or if it was just pounding through her veins faster. It felt as though the blood that coursed through her veins was mingled with Bren's—maybe that was why it ran so hot.

Finished, she and Bren lay perfectly content, utterly satisfied. Aware only of each other, they drifted off to sleep.

Moira awoke deep in the night to find Bren studying her in her sleep. It was then that she realized they were on the floor. Just as it crossed her mind, Bren said it. "Yer uncomfortable," he stated. When he lifted her it was with the ease of a child lifting a doll, then he placed her on the bed. In bed with her they discovered they fit together like a single wave can instantly meld with the sea. Their passion consumed them again, this time being much more deliberate, savoring their love and each other.

When dawn broke Moira was afraid they would not have much time before Daisy and Jeb would be there. This time Bren was asleep, sound asleep. She propped herself on her elbow, wondering at Bren's deep tranquillity. Was this kind of deep sleep even possible for him in the wild? He looked like someone who had found peace after a long journey. Her hand lingered on the curve of his jaw and she gently kissed his brow; he stirred. Never opening his eyes he drew her close to him. Moira sank into his arms; company be damned! At that moment she could care less who came in her cottage. As long as he wanted to hold her, she wanted to be held and would do nothing but revel in it. That's when the need hit her. The need to ensure that he would always be there. She was beginning to understand that it had nothing to do with her or anyone else why Bren left. Bren left because of Bren. He was a wild creature and when whatever it was that told him to leave spoke to his heart...he would go without a second thought. She set her mind that she would find a way to put that second thought into his mind.

Of course, it was the simplest of spells. A lover's tree was really a form of divination. The lovers, in order to see the fate of their love, would plant a tree. A tree meant to be a secret romantic meeting place, or to have special significance to the couple in some way. As this tree grew it would reflect their relationship, if it grew straight and tall, then their love would be just as strong and true…but if the tree grew crooked and sickly, then weak and doomed would be their love. There was a small sapling growing just beyond the sheep's pen. She and Bren would carefully dig it up and relocate it along the sheep path, near the spot she buried Bea.

She tore herself out of bed with zeal for her newfound mission. This was really no more than fortune telling, but Moira planned to add extra care to ensure the tree to be healthy. There was also a way to add extra potency to the deal, to bind the lovers to each other through the tree: If the lovers spilt their blood in the ground along with the tree's roots, then they would be unable to leave each other as long as the tree lived. Moira had never gone that far with the spell, she felt it smacked of manipulation. Controlling someone like that was the opposite of love, she had always said. After all, that was the way Daisy had taught her, not to interfere with someone's free will.

Some of her da's old clothes were ready and waiting for Bren when she coaxed him out of bed. She was already dressed and ready, so she was prepared to fend off his pleas for her to return to bed. Moira would not take no for an answer. "I have some clothes all laid out for ya, and use the rain barrel by the back door to wash up, while I round up the tools we will need to move that tree…."

Out in the shed she gathered the tools they would need to move the sapling tree. She had to look behind the workbench for the hand trowel. "There ya are! Ya pesky but necessary thing!" She began to sharpen the edge of the trowel, much sharper than usually necessary.

Chapter Eighteen

Just as Moira was leaving the shed with her canvas bundle and small shovel, Bren was finishing up at the rain barrel. Moira called, "Grab that bucket and put about two fingers of water in it!"

Bren held up the bucket with a question on his face.

Moira held up two fingers, "Two fingers high from the bottom of the bucket!"

Bren mouthed an "Ahhhh" of assent and turned to the water and the pail. Even when Bren spoke, he got right to the point and said what needed to be said; he never used more words than absolutely necessary. If the situation did not require words he did not use them. It didn't come naturally to him to use language as a primary form of communication. Moira stood watching, considering. Bren's poetry lay in his actions, his movements and his deeds; it came from deep within him, from his soul. And it was visible even when he just lifted a pail. He did not need words.

They headed for the tree. When Moira came to the gate of the sheep pen, she called Gem. As the sheep where milling out the gate around her, Gem came running. Her right hand went up in the air over her head and Gem stopped short, hunkering down close to the ground, all the time looking at her intently, and waiting for orders. Moira snapped her arm as if throwing a ball, except she kept her hand flat and rigid, simultaneously calling out in a low voice, "Deep." Gem understood; that was the signal to keep after the sheep till they were deep in the woods. And then off she went, urging the sheep on.

Bren and Moira knelt by the small sapling, taking great pains to be gentle with the tender roots, and then she wrapped them in an old burlap sack.

They hauled the tree in the bucket up to the grove where Bea rested. First they turned the soil with the shovel. Then Moira began removing earth with her trowel and Bren unwrapped the small tree. He tossed the burlap off to the side, while supporting the small tree with the other hand. Suddenly he felt a stinging sharp pain across the palm of his hand.

"Oh my, yer bleedin!" She put shock in her voice but the concern was genuine. "Oh dear, I must have cut it with the trowel," Moira said, examining the cut while holding his hands over the root of the tree, gently squeezing the wound. Drops of blood fell on the roots of the tree. "Tis not a deep cut, there are some clean rags in the canvas bag with the other tools. I left it back there on the trail. I will finish up here and then we can go back down to the cottage and clean up that cut."

As soon as Bren started toward the bag, Moira turned and sliced her own hand across the palm, letting her own blood spill also on the roots of the sapling. Once the earth was patted firmly around the tree, she too went to the canvas bag to search for a clean rag.

"Are ya hurt too, sweet one?"

He urgently grabbed her hand, but she retracted it, insisting, "Tis just a scratch really," and quickly wrapping her hand to hide the seeping blood. "What did ya just call me?"

Bren paused for a moment to think; those words had come so naturally that he had to think about it. For in his mind, he had always called her that. "Sweet one?"

She nodded her head in affirmation. He took her in his arms, brushed his lips against hers, and explained, "Tis what I have always called ya. When ya were a wee girl, before I heard yer da call yer name, I thought of ya as 'sweet one.' 'Here comes sweet one!' Sounds kind of silly, huh?"

"Why sweet one?" Moira was wrapped in his arms with the side of her face pressed against his chest.

Bren spoke into the top of her hair, "When yer da kissed ya on the forehead, he would smile as if he had tasted something sweet - sweet one! And I wondered at how marvelous ya must taste, and I longed to taste ya too. I was scared though. I didn't know if I would be able to taste the sweetness." He paused and lifted her face to his, kissing her forehead and lingering there. "Just as sweet as I imagined."

She burrowed her face into his chest, crying silent tears.

Chapter Nineteen

As they headed down the trail Moira hummed the "Washing Song," and as they approached the cottage they saw that Daisy and Jeb were also coming round the bend.

"Moira dear, there ya are!" Daisy stopped in her tracks at the sight of a stranger with Moira. Even though she had never met him before, Bren couldn't be mistaken for another. Daisy grabbed the back of Jeb's shirt to tug him back but couldn't hinder his approach, and Bren unconsciously took a few steps back. Lowering her voice, Daisy introduced herself. "Ya must be Bren, it is a pleasure to make yer acquaintance."

Jeb then realized the situation and stood back himself, tipping his hat and giving a silent nod.

Moira led Bren forward just a few cautious steps. "This is Daisy May and her husband, Jeb." Gently she coerced him closer to Daisy. He slowly extended his hand and she whispered, "It's alright." Moira had the feeling that Bren could bolt at any moment as he cautiously shook Daisy's hand.

Very quietly, Daisy initiated, "Pleasure."

"Pleasure." Bren looked from Daisy to Moira, and back to Daisy.

With her free hand she patted his hand, which she was already shaking. "Yer doin fine, luv." It was then she noticed the bloody rag. "Oh dear! Ya have cut yerself, let me see."

It was too much. Bren pulled back a few steps, causing Moira to gently place her hands on Bren's upper arm to steady him, revealing Moira's own bound hand. Daisy May's face darkened. "Blood magic? What's goin' on here?"

Jeb, quite intuitive himself (but not really needing his natural abilities for this), felt the storm coming and made a large "follow me" gesture with his hand, unmistakable to anyone with eyes. "Come along with me, Bren, shall we go inside and see about cleaning up that cut?" Bren looked to Moira for approval, and, placing her hand in his back she gently pushed him on. "It will be alright." Bren followed Jeb with no great speed, but he did follow.

As soon as they were inside and the door to the cottage had shut, Daisy exploded. "*Donna even bother tryin' to deny it.* I can *feel* it, as sure as I can feel a storm! I can *smell* it, as plain as rotten eggs! Countless times I have told ya of blood magic goin' wrong! Leadin' to trouble! Free will should not be tampered with! The Almighty, Himself, gave man free will! Terrible consequences will come of this! A terrible price *indeed*!" Wringing her hands and muttering, suddenly Daisy grabbed Moira by the shoulders and gave her a good hard shake. She demanded, "Tell me now, *what have you done?*"

Moira wrenched out of her grasp defiantly. "We just planted a lovers tree."

"With *blood*!" Daisy was unmistakably yelling now, her voice picking up momentum as it rose in tone. "His blood, and *your* blood, spilt on the *roots*... Oh *Mother of God*!" She trailed off again into muttering, then turned and began to shuffle off. Suddenly she wheeled about and resumed her screams with new fervor. "What possessed ya to try something so foolish? Under *normal* circumstances this spell invites trouble! But *his* blood, Moira...this has never been tried! Never! And I am *quite* sure of *that*! A Selkie's blood…there is no tellin what will happen!"

All the blood drained from her face, and in a whisper, more to herself than Daisy, Moira admitted, "I had not considered that."

"What the *hell* were ya thinkin! The very *best* ya can hope for is that it just fails."

A look of horror spread its white fingers over Moira's already pale face. "It can't fail, it *won't* fail! I will make sure of it."

"Have you not heard a word I said, child! Binding a Selkie to the land is a *cruel* thing." She turned her back on Moira, holding her own head in her hands, but then spun around to point a finger at her niece. "You are runnin' the risk of drivin' him mad! Just like a caged animal he will be! A fox will chew off its own leg when it's caught in a trap! And he will certainly bite *you*, if ya try to help him! Have ya thought about that? What will ya do if he turns violent? What if he hurts ya?"

"Bren would never hurt another person!"

"*He is not a person!*" Daisy paused for effect. "He is not a man, neither is he a seal! He is a Selkie! A *wild* creature, who belongs to the sea!"

Meanwhile, Jeb stepped around Bren as if he were treading on eggshells to gingerly close the door of the cottage. Jeb had already brought in a pail of fresh water. "Some soap and water and a new clean wrapping ought to be all that cut will need." To say Bren was visibly nervous is only half tellin' it. He kept shifting his eyes from the front door to Jeb to the back door, as if trying to gage which exit he could make in the fewest steps. Jeb crossed to the sink, without a word, hoping Bren would find some ease in the silence, though they could hear Daisy's muffled agitated voice, which did not help. Jeb made a lather in a bowl, while Bren was still considering the two doors. Jeb spoke in a low voice, speaking very slowly, "Would ya unwrap yer hand, then come over here, then we can wash it. It may sting a little, but I can see yer no stranger to pain." Bren looked at him with curiosity and suspicion. Raising a soapy hand Jeb pointed to his own cheek to indicate where Bren's scar was on himself. Bren touched his scar and nodded his head in affirmation.

"David told me about the fish hook he dug out of yer cheek." Jeb reached, trying to make a connection.

Bren stepped closer to Jeb and the sink. "Moira's father was a kind man."

"Was it in this kitchen…where David got the hook out?"

Bren came closer another step, extending his hand for Jeb to clean. "I don't remember much, really."

Jeb began to clean the wound, carefully, wanting to keep him talking. "Can ya just try to tell me what ya do remember?"

Jeb kept working while Bren, haltingly, did his best. "After I pulled myself to the rocks, it was all black… then I remember being scared. And I remember the pain; I had never felt anything quite like it. When I was here with…David, all I could think about was how to get out, but afterwards I was very…um…grateful. All he wanted to do was help me."

Jeb finished up the new wrap with a neat little knot, smiled, and said, "Now that wasn't so bad, was it? At the rate that is healing, ya won't need to cover it tomorrow."

"Thank you, Jeb." A moment of silence passed between them. "Maybe ya can help me with something?"

"I will help anyway I can."

"What happened to Moira's parents? I mean, I assume they're dead, because I can't imagine anyone voluntarily leaving Moira."

"Yes, they passed away some time ago." Seeing Bren's

confusion return he added, "'Passed away' is just another way to say *died*."

"How, why?" Bren's confusion was still obvious. "One day they were here, the next they were gone. What happened?"

"We weren't given much of the details. 'Twas an accident; they were hit by a runaway cart."

"A cart? Way out here?"

"No, no, no. It happened in town. Moira would know."

"Have you ever seen her face when there's talk of her da?"

"I see what ya mean."

"It's not just pain, tis more… And whatever it is, I don't like it when it happens."

Before Jeb could respond the door crashed open. Daisy's face was red with anger and the exertion of fighting a losing battle. "Tis hopeless; we are leaving, Jeb!" He leaned back in the chair, looking as if he were about to say something, but before he could Daisy came back quite insistently, "NOW, JEB!"

As he rose to make his exit, he placed his hand on Bren's shoulder. "'Twas grand to meet ya, ya take care of that hand now."

"Take care, Bren," Daisy said, a note of sympathy in her eyes.

Bren followed them out the door and put his arm around Moira, who incidentally looked as is she had been drug through a knothole.

They heard Jeb calmly protesting as Daisy shooed him down the road. "What about Moira's cut, shouldn't we see to that, too?"

"She's a big lass! Isn't she now?" was all Daisy May would say as she urged him along.

They crossed the town in silence; Daisy fumed the whole

way. When they reached the caravan, Daisy went in, slamming the door behind her. Jeb could hear her slamming cupboards; he even thought he heard a plate break. As suddenly as she'd gone in she emerged, again slamming the door behind her. She settled with a plunk on the fold out stair, "Well, do ya want to hear the horror of it all or not?"

Jeb took the spot next to her on the stoop. "Here now, it can't be all that bad."

"It damn well can! Every bit of it!" She told Jeb of the blood magic, her uncertainty with the consequences of attempting this tricky spell with a Selkie as the intended. "And further, this does not seem to be an issue for Moira. All she can think of is hangin' on to this one." She swept with her hand, spanning the breadth of the dirt outside the stoop. "No matter the danger to herself!"

Jeb had his elbows on his knees and his head in his hands, his eyes wild. He was totally speechless.

"I have no idea what the consequences will be, I just know it can't be good." Daisy's words ebbed off into a long silence.

Staring into each other's eyes, Jeb spoke, "The decision is yer's."

"Every instinct says this is trouble," Daisy began, wringing her hands again, but couldn't finish.

In response, Jeb's voice was full of concern, asking a question more than making a statement. "Then we should leave first ting in the morning?" He removed his hat to push back his hair, then rested it, cocked, on the back of his head.

"I'm not sure that is the right ting either. Part of why she is so desperate to keep Bren here is that everyone she loves leaves, and if we go now it will only make her that much more desperate. On the other hand, I don't know how to help her anymore—would I only be stayin' out of guilt? Guilt from having left when David died."

"That was *not* our fault!"

"I know that, Jeb, don't ya think I know that? Still, tis something I wish I could change. Not a day goes by that I don't wonder, what if…what if I had fought a little harder?" With tears swelling in her eyes she hung onto Jeb's shirt. "What if!"

Jeb encircled her with his arms, stroking her hair and comforting her with words of the old tongue.

Chapter Twenty

Days went by and Moira tended to the tree every day, making certain it always had enough water and even erecting a small wire fence around it to protect it from her sheep and other grazing animals. But she had changed in the past few days. She didn't start conversations; in fact she didn't want to talk much at all. She'd been losing her temper very easily, even yelling at Gem on more than one occasion. Bren was uncomfortable with the change, but he was unsure what to do, until after a few days he felt compelled to at least try to talk about it.

While they gathered eggs, awkwardly Bren blurted out, "Your Da never had chickens." After a long silence passed he pressed again, "Why, why is that?"

"Da and I do a lot of things differently." Abruptly Moira left the chicken coop, cradling the eggs in her apron. She intended the conversation to end there, but Bren persisted.

"Nor sheep. Your da didn't keep sheep either, did he?" Following her, against his nature he pushed. Even though conversation was not in his nature, he felt Moira's growing pain and wished to help her. Anyhow, Moira was his nature now.

As she transferred the eggs to a basket, Moira said, "Me father supported his family by fishing, through his life on the sea. My life is different, I have made different choices."

Bren placed his hands on her shoulders to calm her. "I'm just wondering why. Why yer da made the choices he did?"

"Get in line! A *lot* of people would like to understand his choices." The anger in her voice was evident.

"I am talking about the animals," Bren said, confused by her surge of emotion.

Moira sat on the old bench against the back of the cottage, letting out a long and labored sigh. "Da told me he did not want to keep animals and form attachments, especially if they died or he had to kill them. He often told me he thought he would not be able to take an animal's life, an animal he had grown to love."

"But aren't fish animals too?"

Moira chuckled. "I asked me da the same question! But he said, 'I love to eat fish; I do not love the fish itself.' Then, he would put me off by sayin' somethin like 'Ya will understand when ya are older.' Well, I'm older, and…I mean I do understand better, but…."

Bren was kneeling in front of her, looking up, expecting her to finish her thought.

She gazed on her lover, wishing that she could help him understand, understand a man even she was having trouble sorting out. "Me father was a lot more complicated than I ever expected. Full of contradiction…" She paused. "Full of secrets…"

Bren shook his head. "I do not understand."

"This is so hard to explain…" Moira let out a groan. "Da hid things about himself from me, from everybody. I was always told he was an only child, and that his parents were long dead. But he was really a settled traveler and did not want people to know who he had been." Moira gained strength from Bren's eyes and continued, "He had a sister and a large extended family. And he kept that from me. He chose to keep that from me."

"Do you want to find this family? They are your family too, right?"

"I don't need to look, I have known this person my whole life. I loved her every moment of my life, never knowing she was my flesh and blood."

"Daisy?"

Moira nodded her head with tears in her eyes. "And I am angry at him for not tellin me the truth, but I think I understand why he felt he had to…but I thought I had been alone, all this time, and I wasn't. Then I get angry all over again."

"So are ya angry with yer da for the lifestyle he chose or the lyin' part?"

Moira stopped to consider for a moment. "Before now I thought it was just the lyin', but I think by his choosing to live a lie, he also took something from me—he took part of my identity."

Bren slid up to sit on the seat next to her, pulling her close to him in a comforting embrace. "I'm not defending what he did, but… I could always see a sadness in yer da, a sadness that I now know was loneliness." Moira pulled back a little, not breaking the embrace but easing it a little, so she could look into his eyes. Bren continued, "Yes, he choose to live the way he did, but I think that choice hurt himself just as much as it did others. He denied himself his sister's love, he turned his back on his family—it must have hurt him too." Moira's face was buried in his chest, and the sobs came freely now. "Where I come from, how I live, family isn't just important—family is survival. And I think it was wrong what he done. To not tell ya who ya really were, to not tell ya Daisy is yer blood was wrong. I'm just sayin' I think it hurt him too." Bren stroked her hair till she had released all the tears. "I don't think it would be right to leave things the way ya left things with Daisy. Now that ya know she is family, it is now yer responsibility not to send her away again. Gem and I will take the sheep into the hills, if ya want to go find Daisy and Jeb."

Moira blew her nose and washed her face in the rain barrel. She kissed Bren on the cheek. "Thank you."

Starting up the path toward town, she turned and hollered back, "See ya soon!"

Bren nodded, making an "along with ya" motion. As she rounded the corner he sat back down on the bench, a worried look flooding his face. His hands cupped his cheeks, then pushed his hair back tight, a slight groan escaping his lips. "Oh my sweet one, I thought ya were alone, too."

Chapter Twenty-One

Moira crossed town with some fear in her heart; she had shown such disregard for Daisy. She feared what she might find when she reached the campsite. If they were still there, would the argument just continue were it left off, or even worse…what if they had gone! She started wondering how she would begin to search for them, but then came to their camp. When she approached the caravan only Jeb was outside, and, engrossed in a repair, he didn't even notice Moira's approach.

She rested her hand on his shoulder and almost whispered, "Do ya think she will ever forgive me?"

Jeb jumped up with a start, clunking his head on the caravan. He embraced the girl with such fervor that she thought she would pop. "Don't ya know she already has!" He pounded on the side of the caravan and hollered, "Hey you in there, yer wanted!"

Were there tears in Jeb's eyes?

Daisy emerged, grumbling, but stopped cold a moment to see Moira. "Aren't I always wanted for somethin…" They cautiously came together, each considering the other before they fell into each other's arms.

Moira's pleas overlapped with Daisy's words of comfort. Moira said, "I just couldn't lose him, I *had* to try…" Daisy cooed softly into Moira's ear, her hair. "Shh luv, I understand, hush now luv. I understand yer pain."

Daisy led Moira inside. "I will get us some tea." Moira watched her pour the tea, cradling the cup in her hands.

"I have been tortured by somethin ya said..." She couldn't lift her eyes to meet Daisy's gaze, keeping them locked on the swirling tea. "That it was cruel to bind a Selkie to the land." Daisy reached out to her friend's hand, her niece's hand, and slowly Moira raised her eyes and finally met her gaze. Her eyes were so filled with pain that at any moment it could break, but she held it back. It was more important to find a solution now. "I still cannot let him go, but I don't want to hurt him either. Can ya help me do that, Daisy?"

The cups were forgotten and Daisy held Moira's hands as if she were holding on for life, trying to pull a drowning woman to shore.

"How can I undo what I have done without hurting Bren?"

"Can't ya just kill the tree?" Jeb's interjection startled both women, but neither became angry. They knew Jeb could not be far off during such an important conversation concerning his favorite women. Daisy calmly told Jeb what Moira already knew. "Blood magic is a serious business with serious consequences. Under normal circumstances, if the tree's life was ended, both lovers' lives were in grave danger. If one lover takes the life of the tree, then they put the other lover in peril. That's when two human were bound... With a Selkie's blood involved, who knows what the outcome will be."

Moira lowered the cup indignantly. "*Bren*, the Selkie has a name! *Bren*, and I love him, so could we not talk about him like just another ingredient?"

"Sorry luv, I did not mean to be insensitive."

"Oh what am I to do, is it beyond hope!" As they left, Moira slumped heavily on the steps of the caravan.

"Don't lose hope, dear; let's go take a look at the tree, maybe something will occur to us that hasn't before."

On their way to the cottage Jeb hummed a tune so familiar, yet not. Every time he hit a familiar strain and Moira thought she'd almost recognized it, the melody shot off in an unexpected direction. It was a welcome puzzle to distract her thoughts from her seemingly hopeless situation.

Reaching the cottage, there was no sign of Bren. Daisy and Jeb, concerned, looked to Moira and offered, "Bren must still be up in the hills with Gem and the sheep." Moira broke away and ran up the path into the wooded hills, Jeb and Daisy following at a distance.

Ahead they heard Moira's plaintive voice calling out to Bren intermittently, but then, ripping through the wood, Moira let out a blood-curdling scream. They ran forward to find Moira collapsed on the ground, unconscious. Gem was licking the face of his prostrate mistress, and as Daisy tried to revive Moira Jeb spotted what was left of Moira and Bren's lovers tree. He called Daisy May's attention to it. Withered and dead, it was almost beyond recognition—as if the very life were sucked from it.

Chapter Twenty-Two

Daisy and Jeb were able to revive Moira. Barely functioning, her eyes unfocused, she kept repeating, "Tis just not possible…"

Daisy turned to Jeb. "We better get her back to the cottage!" They got the lass to her feet, taking one arm each. Reaching the cottage they lay Moira out on the bed. Brushing Moira's hair from her face, Daisy tried to calm her. "Ssh child, sshhhh. Jeb, dear!"

"What can I do?"

"She is beyond all reason. Maybe, if I can get her to rest… Check in that cabinet there for some whiskey."

"Will do."

After much banging and some clatter, Daisy whispered, "Serves me right for asking a man to find something in a woman's kitchen."

"Not a drop!"

Daisy had some money stashed in her slip, in a special pocket she herself sewed in there for such times, and she handed it to Jeb. "Go to the pub and get a bottle, and be quick about it." As Jeb closed the door, Daisy turned to check the kitchen herself. "I can't believe I just gave me husband money and sent him to buy liquor. I did do that, didn't I?" Not finding any herself, she did find the tea, and set about making a pot.

Taking a warm mug to Moira, Daisy said, "Here luv, take a sip of this, it will help calm your nerves."

Moira drank a sip. "You don't understand, Daisy, you don't understand!" Daisy prodded her to take another sip. "That tree was fine yesterday. What do ya think this means?"

"It looked like the tree's life had been taken out it, all limp like a rag doll it was."

Daisy's expression went from puzzlement to actual fear. "We are dealing with unnatural forces here, stuff that should not be meddled with."

Moira sat up. "Is there any sign of Bren? Could he be hurt? Maybe he needs our help."

"Just lay back, and calm yourself dear, I am sure Bren is fine." The truth was that Daisy feared for all of them.

We join Jeb just as he entered the pub, his eyes taking a moment to adjust from the daylight outside. It was dank and musty inside, and very smoky. Jeb smiled to himself as he wondered if, in the dead of night, hours after the last customer has left, if there was not still a thick cloud of smoke. He too enjoyed a pipe now again, but…to sit in it like this… He let out a cough at the thought.

Just as his eyes adjusted the publican from behind the bar addressed him. "We have no knives for you to sharpen today, so be along with ya, tinker!"

Something in the pit of Jeb's stomach hardened, his stance widened as he braced himself. Then he heard Daisy May's voice in his head, "Be quick about it!"

Jeb swallowed the pride. "Please sir, I only want a bottle of whiskey, and I have money." He placed his money on the counter.

"And where did ya steal that from!" The publican chuckled as he pulled a pint. The old man at the end of the bar snorted, enjoying seeing Jeb taunted.

Daisy was there again, though. "Be quick now!"

"Now there's surely more than enough for a bottle here!"

"All the ways yer sort gets money amounts to thievin' anyway, don't it!" the whole pub was laughing at Jeb now, except... a familiar voice.

"Come *on*, Derm!" Jeb was very happy to have an ally in Sean.

Grumbling, Dermit reached under the bar, producing a half-empty open bottle to Jeb, and proceeded to scoop up all the money on the counter.

Sean had irritation in his voice and grit in his teeth. "*Dermit...*"

"That's all he is gettin, and he is lucky for that!" He glanced around, confident in his supporters. "I would watch myself if I were you, Sean, me boy."

"Come on, Jeb!"

As they exited the pub, Dermit retrieved an unopened bottle from under the counter and, breaking the seal, he poured the old man at the end of the bar a few fingers in his glass. "It's on me, Eamon." The two of them shared the last laugh.

Outside, Jeb thanked Sean, "Tis a good deed ya done, for Moira's sake!"

"What do ya mean Moira's *sake*!"

Jeb gave him a brief description of her state and they didn't stop running till they burst through the door of the cottage.

Daisy was a tad surprised to see Sean and gave Jeb a perturbed look. "I sent ya after a bottle, I didn't expect ya ta come back with half a bottle and this one in tow!"

Jeb was out of breath. "Now see here, if it hadn't been for Mr. Murphy here, I-I...wouldn't have gotten here as quick as I did. I would have gotten the whiskey eventually, but decidedly not as fast." Jeb firmly held his last bit of dignity, and wouldn't let go.

Daisy grabbed the bottle from Jeb and held up her hand to keep them in the kitchen. She poured a dollop in Moira's tea and sat on the bed. "Drink this luv. Don't fret, just sleep."

After a short time, Daisy returned and whispered, "Outside, the pair of ya. Rest is what she needs."

Once the door was closed, Sean was quite insistent on getting to the truth. "Who did this to her? If that man hurt her in any way, I'll kill him!"

Daisy grabbed him by the upper arms. "There is no *man*, Sean!"

"I have seen him with my own eyes, Daisy!"

Daisy knew that what she said next had to be big, big enough to distract Sean from his suspicions and to distract him from the truth. So Daisy blurted, "Moira has had a bit of a shock. Ya see I am not just a concerned friend...I am Moira's aunt."

Silence, even with the cottage between them and the sea, they could still hear the waves crashing on the shore.

Sean was shocked, and Daisy hoped it was enough to throw him off the scent. "But, I don't understand...my family has known Moira's ma's family forever, and her da was an orphan or somethin..."

Half under her breath, Daisy mumbled, "Or somethin."

Sean, still not sure which end was up, tried to make sense for himself. "Moira's grandmother would not have let her daughter marry a traveler!"

Daisy's anger at the lie she'd had to live started boiling anew. "There is the root of it, now isn't it!"

"Daisy May!" Jeb said harshly, catching both Sean and Daisy's attention. Seldom was Jeb ever harsh. "Yes, he lied for his own sake and he lied for Ann's sake. It started that way, but then I think it became to be about Moira." Jeb sighed. "I hated the lies too. But Sean, ya saw how I was treated today; did I have that comin'? Did I deserve that?"

"No, sir, ya did not."

"And Daisy, do you remember when ya were just pregnant with Thomas, not even showin' yet, and we were run out of that town."

"Yes, dear."

"It wasn't only rotten fruit they threw that day!" A silent pause passed. "I don't agree with how David did it, but I understand wanting a better world for yer kids. I do understand."

Chapter Twenty-Three

After much debate they decided that Daisy would stay the night with Moira, and Jeb would walk Sean home, then head on over to the caravan himself. In the morning Daisy woke to find Moira had already made a pot of tea and was slumped over her cup, looking half dead.

Daisy managed a hoarse, if heartfelt, "Good morning, luv."

At first Moira stared coldly over her cup, but on second thought she replied, "I don't know that I would be calling it all that." To say her delivery was deadpan is putting it mildly.

Daisy pulled up a chair and a second cup and put her arm around Moira. "Now that ya have yer wits about ya lass, can you tell me what happened yesterday? What do ya remember before ya collapsed?"

"I was hoping you could explain it all to me, me head's still spinnin."

"Just take yer time, child, take all those images and try to put them together and tell me what happened, as best ya can remember…"

Moira rose and paced, anguish in her face. After a moment she returned to her chair and took Daisy's hand from across the table. "When I got back from our talk yesterday, Bren nor Gem was any where. They were taking the sheep up when I left, so I went into the hills to look for them." She paused for a moment, running her hands over her face, "I was calling for them, and that's when I found it. The lovers tree." Squeezing Daisy May's hand, she continued, "The tree was fine yesterday, it didn't even look a little wilty around the edges. It was like all the life had been taken from it, sucked out of it." Again she rose, as if just recounting the story was enough to alarm her all over again. "I am afraid for Bren." She turned from Daisy, wringing her hands.

Daisy interjected. "Bren can take care of himself, tis you I am worried about."

Moira spun around, she had the most peculiar look on her face, almost annoyance. "Ya don't think *I* can take care of meself?"

"Fine!" She leaned across the table. "Fine, if I were a little girl who just lost both of her parents at once, that would be one thing," standing straight again, "but I am not! I am a grown woman who has been—"

She was interrupted by Daisy clucking her tongue, almost a whisper compared to Moira's near yelling. "Just look at the state of ya, just look will ya."

Moira looked down at her disheveled clothes she'd slept in the night before, then her hands went up to the wild hair created by a night of fitful sleep. Then she noticed her small cottage. The wind abruptly taken from her sails, she plopped into a kitchen chair. "What is happening to me?" she mumbled.

"Well for starters, when Jeb and I found ya, ya were a babbling, muttering *mess*! We got ya back to the cottage here and I could not get ya to rest. So Jeb went to fetch a bottle. After Jeb and Sean returned with the whiskey ya did go down.... But all night you tossed and turned as though ya were tusslin with the devil himself."

"Sean!'" She was back on her feet. "Ya didn't tell him about Bren, did ya?"

"Give me some credit, lass, but I do believe he strongly suspects, I do not believe he could ever imagine what's really goin' on."

"He is just bein' nosy."

"I don't know about that. Ya might be right though, even when he was little he loved puzzles. This just may be another puzzle to work out. I don't know though, that was real concern he had in his eyes for ya! Tis true you can see what a man holds in his heart through his eyes."

"Oh Sean is just bein' Sean!" The notion was easily dismissed by a wave of her hand, but Daisy was not so easily convinced. Moira continued, "I can't keep livin' this way. Lately I feel so confused. Sometimes I feel like an onlooker of me own life, does that make sense, Daisy?"

"Oh darlin', I have felt like that before, but ya have to remember, it is never too late to take on yer own responsibility. It is never too late to take control of yer life. If ya feel out of control it is because ya gave that power away. Don't be afraid to take that power back!"

Daisy's words seemed too simple to be true, but they rang with the clarity of truth. They spent several moments in silence, while Moira organized her thoughts. Suddenly Moira stood up and put on fresh clothes, brushing her hair and pinning it back were the final touches. Daisy just stood there curiously looking on, as Moira began whisking around, picking up as she went. "Well are ya just goin to stand there or are ya going to do those dishes for me!"

"Of course I will, luv." By the time she finished the last dish and looked up from the sink, the cottage was neat and tidy. The turf fire glowed as ever, but even the fire seemed to have a new determination to it.

Moira was clearing the last cobwebs from her kitchen when

she turned the broom on Daisy. "Now scoot!" she laughed, jokingly trying to sweep up Daisy's feet. "Ya have been playin nursemaid to me too long already. Now go home, nurse Jeb for awhile, he'll love it!" Moira quickly embraced her, giving her a peck on her cheek. "I will be fine, and later when the sun is setting, I will come to the caravan and we will have supper together."

"I will go only if yer sure!" she said. In response, she scooted Daisy unceremoniously out the door and up the path.

With the sheep taken care of, Moira hung up some freshly washed laundry. She did not hear his approach, but when she felt the warm familiarity of him, she knew it to be Bren. She leaned back into his embrace without turning around. His hands stroked her abdomen, making their way to her thighs. He began to place kisses on her neck, in the manner of the first few droplets of a gentle spring rainstorm.

His voice seemed extra husky. "I love it when I find ya hanging laundry." The rainstorm of kisses resumed on her neck, a small sigh of pleasure escaped her lips as his hands continued on their given course. "If I had known ya would start laundry after ya came back from Daisy's caravan, I would have come back earlier!"

She broke the embrace, then spun around with her hand on his chest—elbow stiff—to establish some boundaries. She stared at Bren; a hard stare. A stare of disbelief at the words she had just heard. Several moments passed between them, along with an immense silence.

Bren broke the silence. "What? What's wrong?"

She spoke very slowly, very deliberately, "I came back from the caravan yesterday. It has been a full day since I went to find Daisy."

Bren was very emphatic in his disbelief. "That is not

possible! I just left a few hours ago." He took a few steps back. "Gem and I took the sheep up, then I wanted to go for a short swim, I don't understand how this…I was so sure it was a short time." He tugged the hair away from his face, as if that act would somehow make things clear. "It only felt as if I were gone a short time!"

"Time is not measured by feelings, it is measured by the sunrise and sunset!" She was obviously annoyed.

"Time can be measured?" He wore a look of desperation and confusion.

Moira softened when she looked into his eyes. "I came back and you were gone, I didn't know…I didn't know if you were hurt or…dead."

He closed the space between them quickly with long strides, and enveloped her in his arms. "Can ya ever forgive me for causin' this heartache?"

She stood on her tiptoes, grabbing the sides of his head and kissing him aggressively, passionately, with intent. The intention was to quench her now growing desire for him; though the passion also served another purpose. An alternative purpose. His knees grew weak and he stumbled, losing his footing. With her hands on his shoulders she slammed him against the closed cottage door. Her body pinned him against it like a wave crashing to the shore.

"I already have forgiven ya…" She breathed, unlatching the door, and they tumbled into the cottage. Half of her clothes were already gone, buttons popping, but she had little time to worry about such things. They were still not far from the door when, with one swift kick, she slammed the door shut. It did not take much to stir Bren's lust and he removed his clothes in a similar fashion. As they tugged at each other's clothes they scooched across the floor toward the bed. They never actually make it the bed, but came close enough for Moira to grab the side for leverage. The bedclothes came off the bed in her hands as she collapsed in exhaustion on top of Bren. They rested under the covers for but a moment and the love making resumed, the intensity only growing. The afternoon and evening were lost, but given willingly.

The sun set and the moon was high, and the lovers had finally found the bed. Moira sat up and playfully straddled her lover, leaning down to whisper in his ear. "I want to make love to ya in the sea."

Bren pulled her away, unsure. "I do not understand what ya are asking."

"I understand you are not a man. I want ya to make love to me in yer home, in the water."

With the question in his voice, he breathed, "Outside?"

She leaned into his ear again, her lips brushing the lobes wetly. "No one will see, tis dark…"

He scooped her out of bed and dashed out the door. She felt the cold water splashing her as Bren began to wade into the water, the water that was swallowing her body.

As he lets go of her body he said, "Squeeze me neck tightly, and do not let go."

The water rose to her shoulders, but it didn't go any higher even though it felt as if they were still moving. It was painfully cold at first, but as she relaxed, her body seemed to get used to it. Bren faced her outward to the expanse of the sea, and she could not tell were the sky ended and the water began—the horizon was a beautiful blue blur. She felt Bren's body gently beckoning her forward. "How far out are we?" Bren stopped his slow progress out to turn her to face the shore. She let out a gasp and wrapped her legs around his waist.

He chuckled. "I won't let anything happen to ya, sweet one!"

"The shore looks so far away."

"I know exactly were we are, and I know what to expect from these waters. Ya are safe with me."

She kissed him almost before he finished. Quickly he became the aggressor and she was engulfed by his passion. Their love, their bodies became as fluid as the water that surrounded their bodies. Once he slid inside her it felt as easy and as necessary as breathing the way their bodies pushed and pulled against each other.

"Take a deep breath," Bren whispered in her ear. She took the breath, and she felt Bren's hands move to her back as they sunk below the water surface. They began to barrel roll, never losing their personal rhythm. Bren's hands went up her back and out her shoulders. Once his hands covered her own, he broke them from his neck and holding her hands, stretched their hands far over their heads then sweeping their arms to their sides. Repeating this motion they climbed to the surface. Just when she was sure her lungs would burst they exploded into the surface. As they broke the surface they gasped for air. Bren grabbed Moira's wrists and before they bobbed down again he had wrapped her arms around his neck. This time they only went under a few moments, when they surfaced a second time they continued to gasp for air. Their union soon came to a climax and Bren began to make a throaty noise that developed into a beller. They made their way back to the beach. Once inside the cabin they collapsed on the bed. Bren managed to say, "I dreamt of being with ya in that way countless times, but I never dreamt it could feel like that…"

She kissed his brow. "I love you, Bren, as no other."

"And I love you too, sweet one." He feel asleep in her arms. She waited a moment, then wriggled out of his arms.

Moira reached deep under the bed, found what she searched

for, and hauled out a sealskin. A Selkie skin to be more accurate, Bren's skin. She then grabbed her sewing basket, laid the skin out on the kitchen table, then produced the scissors. She then prepared to make her first slice. But she noticed the handheld mirror she had stuffed in the basket along with the scissors after she cut Bren's hair. And she almost did not recognize herself. She looked at her lover, then the reflection, and finally down at the skin laid out before her. She stepped back from the table. She was startled when she heard the clatter of the scissors as they hit the floor.

    She crossed to the bed, curled next to Bren and entered a peaceful sleep.

Chapter Twenty-Four

I need to back up. Do you remember that yesterday Moira promised Daisy she would meet her back at the caravan for supper? Well when the sun was set and still no Moira, Jeb and Daisy began to get nervous. Jeb finally said, "After you went to all the trouble of making a fresh pot of soup, I'll just go fetch her!"

"Ya don't need to do that; she is not comin'. Now eat this bowl of soup before it gets cold," Daisy said in a quite matter-of-fact manner.

"Don't be silly woman! I'll just—" She cut him off, grabbing him by the elbow.

"She'll be busy with him, he's come back, ya know! Can't ya smell it?"

You can well imagine the look Jeb gave Daisy! "Smell *what*, exactly?"

"The magic, Jeb! The magic! Can't you smell it?"

"Does it smell like old socks? Cause all I can smell is your soup!" He sidestepped her arm as she as she swung her old wooden spoon. "Maybe it would help if ya told me what *MAGIC smells like*!"

"It doesn't smell in the traditional sense, it doesn't smell like food cookin' or like flowers. Tis more complicated than that!"

Jeb raised his eyebrows, a silent *well*.

"It's like, it's like…" Daisy jumped when she realized how to explain it. "Tis like the way the air smells after a rainstorm, or the way the air smells when rain is comin'! Like everything is energized."

"Ya have gone round the bend this time!" Jeb was uncertain of whether or not to believe his wife this time.

"Jeb, just try it! Close yer eyes and tell me ya can't smell it too!" Daisy urged.

Jeb closed his eyes and breathed deeply. At first he was making a comical face to get Daisy riled up, but then his face was overtaken by shock and awe. He got a little frightened then perhaps for himself and Daisy, as well as Moira.

Daisy chided him, "I tried to tell him, but he can't even understand the simple truth when it comes from me."

"You scare me sometimes woman, the simple truth." Jeb whipped his pocket rag over his brow then replaced his hat, muttering under his breath, "I hope she knows what she is doin'."

"Sit down then, how about some soup?"

Chapter Twenty-Five

As the sun came up, life blossomed on the beach. With her eyes still closed, her hand searched the other side of the bed. Moira knew before she opened her eyes that Bren was gone. Her eyes opened slowly, she could still see the depression in the sheet were he had been. She wondered to herself, "How long will it be this time?" A small tear escaped and rushed to her pillow as she closed her eyes again. She reflected on the events of the night before, but did not wallow. A decision is made, silently, but written in stone. She got herself out of bed, and got ready for the day.

A hesitant knock came through the front door, and as she stripped the bed she hollered for Daisy to come in. Daisy was pleased to find Moira having a much different reaction to Bren's absence than she had last time. A little confused, she was not quite sure if Moira was being sensible or had gone completely round the bend this time.

Testing the waters she said, "You…you seem so…calm."

Moira responded briskly, "The sheets still need to be washed, now don't they." She stuffed the sheet in the basket of laundry. "Start the tea Daisy, I will start these and be back in a moment." She hoisted the basket and out she went.

She returned when the kettle of sheets had begun to warm. "I will have an extra sugar today."

"Rough night, egh?" Chuckling, Daisy snorted and gave a knowing cackle.

Moira asked, "Who am I, Daisy May?"

"Why yer Moira Donovan."

"Yes, but who is she?"

"Just because yer da wasn't who he said he was doesn't mean yer not the girl ya've always been!"

"But I'm not!" Frustrated, and a wee bit scared by herself, Moira said, "I got a glimpse of who I am becoming, and I... I don't want that!"

"What are ya sayin', dear!" Daisy registered some alarm.

Moira explained what almost happened with Bren's hide. "When I saw my own reflection... I did not recognize myself. I knew it was me own reflection but I felt like an outsider watchin' a desperate woman. And it was then I decided to control my life and not become that desperate person."

Daisy embraced Moira, her eyes moist. "I am so proud of ya!" She rocked her back and forth, cradled in her arms, for a moment, "What can I do to help you? The road of independence is by its very nature rough. Tell me the plan and what I can do!"

"I am going to need yer help. I remember when I was a child I didn't understand why you and Jeb left at the end of the summer. Do ya remember telling me all your family came together, and all wintered together?"

"Yes, lass..." she said, too late. She was crying.

"I remember wonderin' how great uncles and grandmas were all going to fit in yer caravan. And Da told me it wouldn't be just yers, there would be plenty of other caravans. Everyone would have a place to sleep. It was a time for all the storytellers to come together and share their stories and songs, so that way they could be nourished and grow, the storyteller and the story."

A moment of silence passed between them, broken by

Moira. "I understand ya will need to talk to Jeb…"

"Nonsense! We would love to have ya!" They embraced.

"Will ya help me tie up some loose ends?" Moira had in her hands a list of what she needed to accomplish before she could leave her home by the sea and join her aunt and uncle on the road.

"Of course," Jeb entered the kitchen through the open door, "we can all put our heads together."

"What's this about?" Jeb looked with a raised eyebrow as he pulled up a chair. Daisy and Moira filled him in and they all discussed what things needed to be done, and their options.

Jeb raised his cup to get every last drop of tea before setting it down with resolve. "I will head over to O'Malley's place and see what he will give me for the sheep."

Daisy's eyes widened and she gulped down her tea. "Don't let him talk ya down below what we agreed on here! That O'Malley is a slippery old bastard!"

"I am more concerned they find a good home!" said Moira.

Jeb kissed her forehead, his hat in his hand. "Ya'd think she didn't trust me, now wouldn't ya?" Quickly he made his exit, just in case Daisy had a pinch for him.

Moira watched him leave and adjusted herself in her chair. "I will head over to the Duffy Place, Kathleen Duffy's ma keeps chickens already, maybe she will find some room for mine."

Daisy, already flustered, warned, "Now those are good laying chickens, *do not* accept less than they are worth." She shook her finger at Moira, knowing it would do no good. "I will start clearing this place out to close up for the winter."

A few hours flew by as Daisy began cleaning out cupboards, during which Moira returned with Kathleen on her father's wagon. They exchanged greetings with Daisy, then loaded up the chickens. Once done, the two friends embraced.

Kathleen smiled through tears. "I understand why ya have to go, I am still gonna miss ya though!"

Moira smiled back. "And I you...and I you!"

As Kathleen rode off, Daisy commented, "That Amadon is havin' a jar with O'Malley to close the deal. I have no doubt!"

Daisy and Moira headed back in to the cottage to finish the cleaning out, and soon enough Jeb swaggered in. "Tis done. The deal has been made."

Daisy asked, "So how many jars did O'Malley have to give ya for you to come down to his price?"

Indignant but reserved, Jeb responded, "I got the price we asked for, and no less. And O'Malley didn't give me any jars!" He slid into a kitchen chair, "O'Malley did not want to pay yer price luv, but I held firm—so I left. But on the way back I bumped into old Fitz, Mr. Fitzgerald, and he wanted to buy me a pint."

Daisy rolled her eyes, letting out a huge sigh.

"Strictly business luv, strictly business. Any way, I told Fitz about the fine quality of Moira's sheep, and how O'Malley was tryin to cheat our lass out of a fair price! He inquired as to our 'fair price', and said wouldn't he be happy to buy the sheep at that price! Then he said I could drive the sheep out to his place tomorrow. He would give me half then and there, and half on delivery."

Daisy squinted her eyes.

Jeb continued, "I told him that would not do, that you would skin me alive if I came back with any less than the full amount for Moira. Then he said I was a good man and he knew what it was like cause he had one just like ya at home!" He plunked down the money, which Daisy counted, and was pleased to find all there.

Daisy finished cleaning the counter, then said to Moira, "We will be by bright and early to collect ya, so we best be goin' now."

Moira kissed her aunt and uncle. "Gem and I will have the sheep ready, as well as ourselves."

She knew that the last loose end she had to deal with by herself. No one could help her say goodbye to Bren.

Chapter Twenty-Six

Sean could see Moira spinning with a drop spindle; by the glow of a lantern he watched her twist the wool through the window. Watching the whir of the top-like spindle, he almost forgot his purpose—almost. He waited among the rocks on the beach for the man, this lover who to Sean's thinking was bringing sorrow to his Moira.

Bren's feet made no sound on the sand, but Sean saw the movement. He crouched, ready to spring on the unsuspecting Bren. Sean tackled him, and having the element of surprise, easily pinned him to the ground. He was not shocked by Bren's nudity; in fact he expected it because the first time he saw Bren was on the beach, naked, kissing Moira.

In their struggle Bren lost grip of his hide, and it fell near the struggling men. Sean spotted the soft leather skin and things began to click in his brain. Sean, half whispered, "You are not a *man,* are ya? Yer one of the old ones Moira's da used to talk about!" He grabbed a stone that was easily held in two hands, yet heavy enough to get the job done. "I won't stand by and watch ya devour her heart. This will put an end to it!" He hoisted the stone high up over his head to strike.

"But I love her!" Bren hoped the truth will find the mercy in his attacker's heart, but the only response in Sean was to raise the stone higher.

"And she loves me!"

This did give Sean pause. He dropped the stone and fell from his knees off of Bren, onto the wet sand.

"*Sean!*" Moira's voice startled them both.

As she approached, Sean's feeble defense was, "I only meant to protect ya…"

"Get inside, Bren, I will be right along." Bren grabbed his hide and dashed into the cottage, and as he did Moira turned on Sean. "What did ya think ya were doin?"

"I could not stand seein' ya hurt like that."

"You and I both know this was more about 'Sean' than anything. You were taking the decision out of my hands. It's my life, let me deal with it. Ya wanted Bren out of the way, and ya wanted this so badly ya were willing to take the life of another creature! Killing Bren would not have solved anything! If you had killed him, I would have hated ya for it!"

"But I didn't kill him!"

"What would have happened if I had not come along when I did?"

"I don't know… Moira, I dropped the rock!"

She could see Bren pacing inside and the pain of reality began to creep over her. It coloured her words, and when the bitterness came out of her mouth she instantly felt the pain they inflicted. "Then it's a good thing we'll never know what would have happened. You are positively the most selfish man I have ever met, *Sean Murphy.* Given present circumstances, that's sayin' a lot." Her voice grew louder again. "Save yourself the frustration, just go home, Sean!" Tears clouded her eyes.

"But," Sean pointed to the cottage. "It's not human! What if he tries to steal ya away!"

Moira's rage was greater than he thought she was capable of; she felt like the little girl overhearing her parents argue about her being "whisked" away. Determined not to feel helpless again, she shouted, "Go home, *Sean*! *Now*!" Her tears did not diminish her fury.

As helpless and hopeless as a leaf on the wind, Sean retreated. Her head in her hands as he padded away across the beach, Moira felt as though she was unraveling. She realized that only she could weave her life.

Entering the cottage, Bren instantly engulfed her in his arms. She broke their kiss, the type of kiss that defined their love, and turned in anguish of what was to come.

Her reaction, and the events that had taken place, confused Bren. "Why did he want to kill me?" he said.

"It's very complicated." She thought a moment, and said, "At the same time it's very simple. Too simple."

Understanding, Bren nodded his head. "Are you alright?" She looked deeply into his eyes and her pain was at once his own. As she spoke, the words were unsurprising, for he read the intent in her eyes.

"I have decided to spend the winter with my aunt and uncle on the road. I have sold the sheep and chickens." She paused, resigned to unforgiving reality. "I love you, I always will, but we must end this. Not just because we will be apart, but because we must. Yer soul answers questions in my soul and I feel more complete than ever before. But the fact remains that we will never completely satisfy each other, because you are not a man and I am not a Selkie."

Bren completed her thought, "You must find the answers to your own questions within your own soul." He cradled her in his arms, and said, "I know you will find your answers there. Because that is were I found my answers."

No more words passed between them. In silence they walked to the beach, arms entwined. Where the water meets the

FOR MOIRA'S SAKE

shore they kissed; they kissed as lovers compelled to part.
"I will always love you, sweet one."
"And I you, Bren."
He waded into the water waist high, then he dove forward, going under the water. When the arc caused him to resurface she saw the beautiful Selkie dive again, his tail disappearing in a wave.

Chapter Twenty-Seven

When Moira saw the last woolie tail disappear around the bend, it hit her that she was ending a chapter in her life. The next step was to create a foundation of truth, so the next chapter could be written freely without the pain of lies.

She and Daisy closed up the cottage and covered the windows. Daisy held her niece comfortingly in her arms. "It would be alright to be sad."

Moira replied, "That's just it, Daisy, I am not sad at all! I know I will be back and I am looking forward to going!" She squeezed Daisy back. "I don't think saying goodbye to Gem will be so easy."

As they began down the road, Jeb and Gem met them. Jeb's first words were, "Boy, was Fitz glad to see us with those sheep! I think I saw his wife at the door with a skillet in her hands. A skillet with his name on it if we hadn't shown up! My heart went out to him, it was the look of worry and dread that all married men share."

Daisy hollered as Jeb was still some distance from the caravan, "Wouldn't you be lucky that I'm leadin' this horse and can't chase ya!" She looked over her shoulder and winked at Moira. Moira winked back, and Daisy May was off running.

"Mother of God, help me!" Jeb ran for his very life back the direction he came.

A short time later, Moira could see Sean's house on the approaching crest. She stopped the cart for seemingly no apparent reason, and shouted into the bushes, "Come on, stop actin like moon-eyed kids and mind this horse while I talk to Sean!" Jeb and Daisy emerged from the bushes, Daisy adjusting the line of her blouse. Jeb replaced his hat as if it were a crown of gold.

Moira turned to Gem and clapped her hands, to which Gem jumped immediately to her side. As they made their way up Sean's path, she worried about how he would react to her. Things were said the night before that couldn't be unsaid, and even if she apologized for calling him selfish, the pain of it hearing it could not be taken back. Besides, to some degree, it was true. Even she had to admit there was good cause to doubt her judgement lately though. She settled on knocking on the door and letting whatever happened happen. Finally she knocked, and before she realized that the door was open Sean scooped her up in his arms and twirled her around the room.

"I am so glad you are here! That ya didn't run off with him!" He set her down. "And you're right, I can be a selfish Amadon—but I was so scared for ya!" He never took a breath. "But ya are right, I am a meddler when my own interests are at stake; I try to control things, but I love you so much!" He shocked himself with the words. He had not intended to say them, they had just came tumbling out.

Moira looked into his eyes and saw the child Sean had been in their youth, then she saw the man he had become, then she noticed he had bags under his eyes…he didn't look like he had slept and he'd not shaven.

Her hand stroked his whiskers. "Do you know how long I have waited to hear ya say those words to me?" His hand covered hers and she continued, "And now I'm…I'm leavin'."

Her hand slipped from under his. "Daisy May told ya about bein my da's sister, right?"

Looking like he had just been punched in the gut, Sean slumped down in to a kitchen chair, "But Moira, that does not make a difference to me!"

"But it makes a difference for me."

"I don't understand? Why?"

"All my life, Sean, I have felt like somethin' was missin'. Like everyone else had all the answers and I had no clue where to begin. Now I have the chance to meet a whole family I didn't know I had. I have the chance to fill in the blanks that have been missin' all these years." As Sean still looked disappointed and confused, she continued. "I'm not lookin to become someone else, I want to find me."

"How long is it going to take to find you?"

"I don't know that. It's not like I have a road map or anything." An awkward silence passed between them, and so Moira spoke again. "I sold the chickens to Mrs. Duffy and the sheep to Mr. Fitzgerald."

Sean went pale; the sale of the animals meant there was no turning back. "Yer really goin'?"

"See Sean, the family winters together, everyone shares the same campground. If I leave now with Daisy and Jeb, we can quietly seek out other family members, and people can get used to the idea and accept me. Daisy doesn't think it will be a problem, but I am a little nervous. Sean, I need to ask two favors of ya."

"Anythin, absolutely, anythin!'"

"Could you check on the cottage from time to time? Everything is boxed up or covered and the windows are covered against storm. Just till I get back, just sweep once in a while and make sure no wild animals ravage the place."

There was hope for Sean in any plans for Moira to return. "Wouldn't I be happy to. What else?"

"It's just that I don't think Gem will like the road much, and he is not as young as he used to be." She stumbled at asking this favor; she wasn't quite sure herself just what she was asking.

Sean jumped in. " Wouldn't I love it if Gem stayed on for a bit! Gem's me old pal, he is," he said, rubbing the sides of Gem's head. Gem licked Sean's scruffy cheek. "And wouldn't I be glad to have the extra help I am sure Gem will be."

"Grand! I am going to need to be goin', Daisy and Jeb are waiting for me." She gave Sean a long hug and kissed Gem on the head. He followed as Sean walked her to the edge of the road. They exchanged more hugs, and when Moira began to walk to the caravan she held up her hand for Gem to stay. Gem whined and danced around, not understanding, and so Moira came back apiece and knelt down to his eye level.

"I will be back, it's only for a while," she said.

Sean did not care that she was just reassuring the dog, he needed to hear it too. He lent down and patted Gem. "Don't worry, boy."

"Now stay with Sean, *stay*." Moira was about a quarter of a mile away when Gem was dancing and whining again.

Moira looked back from the caravan, tears streaming down her face, not sure if they were for the dog, Sean, or both. Just then from behind her Daisy waved goodbye and Gem was off like a shot.

To himself, "Smart dog!" then he shouted to Moira, "Don't worry about the cottage!"

She hollered back, "I will write!"

Sean watched till he could see the caravan no more….

About the Author

My name is Cynthia Colleen Murphy Andrews, my friends call me Cindy. I live in a small town in Wisconsin with my husband and two children. I went to Beloit College, in Beloit, Wisconsin, where I earned a BA in Psychology. I have a disorder called Friedrich's Ataxia, because of which I use a wheelchair to get around. Many people see an individual with a disability and all they see is the chair or the cane, ect.. My disability is not who I am. It affects *how* I grocery shop. It affects *how* I get to the post office. My disability *does not* define me. Living with a disability today makes you appreciate how far our country has come in respecting the rights of Americans with disabilities, yet it profoundly highlights where we fall short. I enjoy music, reading and playing chess with my kids. I enjoy sending mail art. Oh, and I enjoy writing, too.